DEDICATION

This book is dedicated to the memory of my brother, Fred O. Montoya in appreciation for his lifelong friendship, encouragement and inspiration. He lives forever in my heart and memories.

Copyright © 2009 Joseph F. Montoya

All rights reserved.

ISBN-10: **1483944514**
ISBN-13: **978-1483944517**

Acknowledgements

Ted Montoya, Candy Crawford Kunz and Tiffany Jarvis, Tom Gee, Rhonda Palmer, my wife Mary, Marci Harris, Lorie Harris, my mom Lucy Montoya and Marion Montoya, Eloise J. Harle, Ray and Marlene Wolfe, Shelly Montoya, Helga and Jimmy Marr, Don Jones, Richard Merriman. Thank you and all those who have contributed to my books. Thank you all.

TO THINE OWN SELF BE TRUE,
AND IT MUST FOLLOW, AS
NIGHT THE DAY, THOU
CANST NOT THEN BE FALSE
TO ANY MAN.
WILLIAM SHAKESPEARE

Where is Brian Douglas?

CHAPTER ONE

I was jolted awake. As I listened I became aware of a steady vibration and the roar of an engine. It didn't sound like a car, then it hit me…it was an airplane. A friend had taken me for a ride in a small plane once and this sound was the same. This plane was bouncing around and I was groggy, weak, uncomfortable and felt like barfing. I could hear voices, people talking and laughing. When I tried to move I discovered I was wrapped up and tied in something, maybe carpet or tarp---but whatever it was, it wasn't warm. I coughed.

"Hey George I think our man woke up," someone hooted.

"Listen brain dead, I told you not to use names," George hissed angrily. "Check him out and see if he's awake."

A man reached over the seat and shined a light in my face. I pretended I was still out and he turned around.

"I guess he's not awake. I heard him cough and thought he might be waking up."

"Hey George, are you sure we're going to be able to open the door and, and, you know?" a third person queried.

"Stop with the names, Dumbo. Yeah we'll be able to pitch him out easily even in this stupid weather. Hell, maybe we'll drop you out too." Several people laughed. I could feel the plane bucking through the turbulence as we flew on.

"How far are going to take him into the mountains?" someone asked.

"If you ask me that question one more time I'm going to throw you out too. Do you understand that, you cry baby?" George barked.

"What's with all the fuss about our names? This guy is going to take a dive out of an airplane into some very snowy, cold mountains and you think he might live to tell someone about it? You gotta be kidding. If he doesn't die from the fall, he'll freeze to death and if he doesn't freeze to death he's going to have about a hundred miles to walk out of these mountains. He'll never make it!"

"Bart's right. Who's going to live through that," George shouted just as they hit another bad pocket of turbulence.

"Hey George, are you sure you can get us back to Wenatchee through all this crap after we unload this guy?"

"You better hope I can. Even the 747's have trouble in this weather. All right guys, we're going to circle around and you can bring our man up to the door. Bart, you open it and you and Tom push him out when I tell you."

The three men wrestled with the man's body and got it to the back seat.

I knew I was going to die and wanted to plead for my life, but knew it was hopeless. I would die a man, as I had lived. It would all be over very soon. I started praying silently.

"OK, Tom open the door," George yelled.

Just as Tom opened the door the plane hit a pocket and jerked abruptly to the right. He sailed out into the frigid air. It happened so fast Tom didn't utter a word, and the rest of the men just stared blankly at each other. No one said a word.

"It was an accident," George yelled, "get yourselves together and do what we have to do."

I felt the cold wind hit my face.

"What about the head cover we were going to put on him?" Bart asked.

"Forget about it," George said as he turned toward me to see the progress.

I opened my eyes, looking directly into George's, then at Bart.

"I'll see you again you bastards," I yelled defiantly.

"Get rid of him," George shouted over the wind whistling through the open door.

I felt my weightless body rocketing toward the ground through the cold air and started to pray.

CHAPTER TWO

I felt heat and saw the flickering light of a fire dancing on the ceiling of what appeared to be a cabin. How could that be? I was sure I had died. When I tried to move I felt like I was incased in concrete. There was no movement. I knew only one thing, the pain was worsening by the second. I hurt all over. When I tried to move my eyes, the muscles around my head hurt. My eyes welled with tears. I was alive. I couldn't believe it, but I was feeling sorry for myself. I was crying and couldn't stop. Then it dawned on me that I couldn't hear anything. I could see the reflection of light on the ceiling but I couldn't tell what it was or where it was coming from; probably from an open fire or a wood stove, I thought.

How did I get here? I screamed in my head.

Tears ran down my face and I could feel them burning a path as they ran down. My face must be raw, I thought.

I had been asleep, but for how long, I wondered. The fire was throwing patterns of shadows dancing on the ceiling. I tried to move again, maybe there was a window and I could at least determine the time of day. I had the sensation that I had moved my fingers, wherever they were, but I couldn't be certain. Where was whoever brought me here? I was hungry. How long had I been here? I fell asleep again and when I woke I could see a faint shimmer of light to my right, possibly some kind of lantern or a candle. Who could have found me and brought me here? I was now in a bed or cot. Whoever it was meant for me to stay alive…I think. I tried to move. I couldn't.

Oh my God! What if I was a paraplegic? I imagined myself in one those motorized wheel chairs, like Christopher Reeves. I might as well be dead. I felt a surge of tears rolling down my face, and wanted to shout 'why.' I hated feeling sorry for myself. I don't customarily swear, but right now I was mad as hell and wanted to curse. I hated what was going on with me. I stopped. That's right…I could feel the tears burning my face again, of course. That meant I had some sensation, which meant

I could feel things, yeah but, how about my body? What could be wrong with my body and did the person who brought me here know I couldn't move? I wondered if it was possible to feel your face but not your body. I was hungry. I lay there thinking about being hungry. Is it possible to feel hunger if your body is stone?

I fell asleep again and dreamt I was walking on live, red-hot coals. I felt them burning the bottom of my feet and screamed, "Ahhhh." Seconds later I was staring up into the smiling face of a large oriental man. He grunted and said something I didn't understand and showed me a piece of wood that was lit like a candle. He was muttering in his language as he moved toward where my feet might be. I felt heat on my foot and groaned. Again he leaned over me and smiled.

I think I understood what he had done to me. I tried to say something but I couldn't. The yellow-faced man had disappeared.

I was not a piece of stone. I must have feeling in my feet and most probably, my body. When he put the lit wooden candle to my foot I must have raised my head slightly because I was aware of not only the heat, but also the sounds around me. I could hear now.

He was humming to himself. I tried to lift myself up to see what he was doing but was so weak I could hardly move. I lay there wondering what he could be doing when the aroma hit my nose. He was cooking and I was suddenly ravenous.

A few hours later he lifted me and put an animal hide behind my head and shoulders. I was aware of how strong this man was by how little effort he exerted. He placed a stool next to my bed and came back with a wooden bowl of carrots, potatoes and bits of meat. He spooned out a chunk of potato in heavy broth, blew on the portion of dripping stew and then helped me open my mouth by putting his large thumb on my chin. He spooned the warm spud in my mouth. I chewed twice and swallowed. When I began coughing he nodded, smiling, said something in a foreign language and walked away. Less than two minutes later he was back with the bowl, this time with only the broth, which he spooned slowly into my mouth. When I finished that bowl he brought another. I ate two bowls then, promptly threw up. He cleaned up the mess and gave me a small drink of water. I moved my legs and got the feeling you get when your legs or arms fall asleep; that tingling feeling. I opened my mouth to talk, but nothing came out.

The large man looked at me and smiled, said something I couldn't understand and walked away.

I felt pretty good. I had eaten and drank some water. I looked up at the ceiling of the cabin and dropped off to sleep.

When I woke up the wind was howling outside and I wondered what time it was. Not that it mattered, but it was my first thought. Where was he? How big was this cabin? Was he the only one living here? Where in the world was I? How long had I been here? How did I get here?

The man's head came into my field of vision. He spoke to me, but I didn't understand a word he said.

He threw the blankets off my body, reached down, lifted me up and sat me over to a chair, then left the room. My chest hurt like hell when he set me down. I groaned and noticed I was buck-naked. My left arm and right leg had make shift casts of half inch cedar secured with white bandages. It looked as though the bandages were real. My left foot was covered with the toes exposed. Maybe my host was a doctor of some sort.

I tried to look around but my neck hurt when I moved ever so slightly. I felt strange sitting at a compromising angle where my jewels were exposed to anyone that entered the room. Maybe I was a modest person, I thought.

I heard the big man off to the left of me. The floor creaked when he walked. He dropped something on the floor and then came into my view, gave me a smile and said something. I just stared at him and he disappeared again.

He returned with a calendar and positioned it where I could see it. Thirteen days had passed and now I was able to climb out of bed; though it was an extremely slow process. My ribs were still very sore. Frankly my whole body was a mess. I was eating like a horse though, thanks to his cooking. He sure knew how to put food together. I was eating potatoes, carrots and something that looked liked stewed tomatoes and occasionally bowl of rice. It was delicious.

I still couldn't tell if he was Indonesian, Japanese or Chinese, nor did it matter. He had saved me and I was indebted to this man for the rest of my life.

Three months had passed and though able to walk, I was not totally healed. My ribs didn't hurt any longer and my right foot was healing. The large man had removed the makeshift cast and I was able to walk precariously, if only for a few steps at a time.

He went about his business as though I wasn't there. prayed then practiced some slow, flowing movements. I also heard him chanting occasionally.

One day I had ventured out for a short walk to the place where I had seen him fetch water from a small creek a short distance from the cabin. There was still snow all around and I shouldn't have tried walking on the slippery surface. But there I was, walking around like a newborn babe and feeling pretty proud of myself when I fell into the frigid creek and hit my head on a boulder. When I woke up I was by the stove at the far end of the cabin.

My benefactor had pulled me from the creek, taken the wet clothes off and laid me down by the warm stove. When I sat up and looked around he handed me a heavy wool sweater and motioned for me to put it on. I wasn't a large man, but I wasn't five feet either, however sliding into that sweater made me feel like a kid playing dress up.

I sat there, looking into the crackling fire, when all of sudden I knew who I was. I shouted out loud, "My name is Brian Douglas," and punched the air as if in victory. "Mr. Man, where ever you are, I know my name," I yelled. "I know who I am." I started crying with joy, placed my hands over my face and sat there sobbing until a hand touched my shoulder. When I looked up at him he handed me a manila envelope. He was smiling like he knew what I had said.

On the front of the envelope someone had written the words: 'To Mr. John Doe.' I thought about those words. Why had he given me this envelope? There was also a pen and pencil in the folder.

I pulled out the letter inside and read it carefully and slowly; it was three pages long, very well written, and especially informative. There was a business card attached, indicating the name and contact information of the author.

So my host now had a handle - - Tom Wah Gee. The author, his nephew, was an orthopedic surgeon. I smiled as the pieces of this puzzle started to fall into place. I looked up to see Tom Gee smiling back as he lifted his right hand and formed a circle with his thumb and index finger. "OK," he said with a big grin, then stood and left the room.

Tom Wah Gee had been waiting for the right time to give me the note. Son Lo Gee was the Good Samaritan who had put me back together after his uncle had found me. I read on, the uncle had witnessed my decent from the low flying plane and plucked me from the avalanche my fall had precipitated. The uncle, Tom Wah, had estimated that I had plunged approximately a thousand feet. The only reason I had survived the fall from such a height was that I had fallen onto the side of a mountain that was steeple steep, with heavy snowfall from the night before. My body never hit the ground flat, but rolled down the mountain on a cushion of snow, causing a small avalanche. When I finally came to a stop I way lying on top of the snow where Tom Wah Gee found and rescued me.

My body had been secured tightly with a heavy tarp which had prevented the snow from peeling my skin right off. I could hardly believe I had lived through that.

I reread the letter. My host, Tom Wah Gee, was a Shaolin Monk. That made sense too. He didn't talk a lot. I thought of the old series on television with the Shoalin Monks, and here I was with a real live one. I was in good hands with Tom Wah Gee. I wondered how long I would remain here. Son Lo Gee would not be back until August, eight months away. Son had not mentioned how he came to this place or how he left. Surely he would not hike into this…this place. Would he?

Dr. Gee's last paragraph read: "Mr. Doe if you are able to read the notes in the envelope I have left for you, I wish you would provide your full name, address and all telephone numbers. I did the best I could with what I had available. I can only hope you will survive. This is for the purpose of notifying your kin, should it become necessary."

That was a sobering thought.

CHAPTER THREE

"Who is it this time?" George Tilden screamed into the phone.

"Please Mr. Tilden, it's one of your friends, Vandy Earhart. Do you want me to tell him you're not here, sir?" the secretary inquired.

"No, no. Go ahead and put him on. I'm sorry I screamed at you, Christina. I'm just having a bad day."

"I understand, sir," she responded cordially, "I'll connect you."

"What's happening, Vandy?"

"I'd like to get together, maybe for lunch. Would that be possible?"

"Sure, how about The Windmill at 2?"

"I'll be there," Vandy agreed.

"Thanks for meeting me, George. We've got a problem and - "

"Sit down, Vandy, Take the load off your feet, and calm down. You're going to have a heart attack. Check out the menu and find something you'd like to eat."

Vandy took a deep breath, relaxed his shoulders and looked at the menu.

"You fellas ready to order?" the waiter asked.

"Yeah, bring us your best steaks, with potatoes and vegetables," George ordered "and two glasses of red wine please."

"Yes sir. How would you like those steaks?"

"Rare."

"Yes sir, I'll be right back with your wine."

"All right Vandy, what are you all up in arms about?"

"It's about Tom Workman. His mother wants to know what happened to him," Vandy stammered.

George nodded as he took a sip of his wine. "What did you tell her?"

"I told her I didn't know anything."

"Good. That was the right answer." George could tell Vandy wasn't comfortable about giving her 'the right answer'. He still had a worried look on his face.

"What do you think we should tell her Vandy?"

"I don't know...I just don't think this is going to go away that easily, George."

"I know Tom was your friend and you feel bad about what happened to him," George stated quietly.

"It wasn't that I knew Tom. He's the reason we knew about...about... "Brian Douglas," George responded, cutting Vandy off. "Do you think we should cut her in on the money? Is that what you're thinking, Vandy?"

"I don't know. What do you think George?"

"Well, for one thing, Mrs. Workman didn't do any of the heavy lifting on this job. We went through a lot of trouble for that money. I used my plane and you guys did all the grunt work. Maybe Tom shouldn't have taken a dive along with our man, but it's too late to cry about it now. It's over and done with. Now go ahead and eat your steak. I'll call Bart and we'll figure out some way to make this all right for you. I might have Bart go and talk to Mrs. Workman. OK? Would that be all right with you?"

"Yeah, I guess. He'd just talk to her, right George?"

"Vandy, I'm hurt that you would think anything else. Of course he would just talk to her! You know Bart well enough to know he wouldn't do anything bad to Mrs. Workman. We're not looking for trouble, Vandy. So far we seem to be in the clear. Right?"

"Well - - I haven't heard anything," he managed to mumble.

"You had a great idea when you came up with the Cascade Mountains, Vandy. Pure genius. I mean drop someone out in the middle of a mountain range and let nature take it's course. Pure genius. Hey, you're not eating your steak. You don't want me to think you don't like having lunch with me. Do you?"

Vandy forced a smile, "Hey George, I love steaks and I am hungry," he swore as he cut a piece of rare meat and popped it in his mouth. Vandy felt guilty taking credit for the Cascade Mountain thing, but hey, Tom wasn't around any more.

George and Vandy walked across the parking lot making small talk, Vandy hesitated when they reached his car.

"We're still going to wait for a year before we distribute the money. Right George?"

"That's what we agreed on, Vandy and I haven't heard anything different. But now we are only three instead of four, and that's a good thing. Don't you think?"

"Yeah that's right George but…you said you were going to talk to Bart about…maybe giving Mrs. Workman some money…right? Don't you think that would be the fair thing to do, and then maybe she would stop with all the questions. Don't you think that would work?"

George looked over at him and nodded. "You know Vandy. You're a very smart man. That makes sense. If we cut her in for a hundred thousand, she just might forget about asking questions we don't have answers for. I'm going to bring this up to Bart and see what he thinks. Can you meet with us to discuss this thing later?"

"I'll go along with whatever you two decide. It's just a suggestion. Whatever you guys decide I will certainly go along with, but if you want me to be there, I'll come."

"OK Vandy. I'll talk to Bart and let you know what we decide."

George Tilden had agreed to meet Bart Colangelo on the loop, which was the trail that circled from one bridge to the other, making a loop from the Wenatchee side to the East Wenatchee side. It was a nice trail for walking, running or bike riding. The Loop always had someone doing one of those three things. During the summer the Columbia River had speedboats, small fishing boats, Kayaks and water skiers galore. The summers in Wenatchee ran from hot to very hot. Right now it was early spring with the chill factor keeping all but the hardy from using the trail. It was a good meeting place for people that didn't want anyone to overhear them.

"We didn't 'get rid' of Tom. He accidentally fell out of the plane. No ones fault. What the hell is Vandy talking about? Giving Mrs. Workman a hundred thousand dollars? Is he crazy? That's just pure bullshit. What do we know about Tom's mother? For all we know she could start blabbing this all around town and then what?"

"Take it easy Bart. Vandy's idea is good. I would like you to go and talk to Mrs. Workman, try to get a feel for what she's like. You pick up on people quickly and I think you could talk to her and see if it would be to our benefit to do what Vandy suggested, that's all."

"Are you through?" Bart shouted as he threw up his arms in disgust. "Well right now, I think it's a bad idea. What the hell does a grieving mother know about keeping her mouth shut? We'll just be opening up a can of worms that we won't be able to close. The next thing we'll be considering is doing away with her, George. Why did Vandy bring this up? He probably should be the one talking to her. He knew Tom better than either of us. I'm telling you George, no good will come of this."

"Hey Bart, no one said it was going to be easy. We've taken care of the hardest part. Now we have to be smart about how we proceed. How hard can it be to talk to Mrs. Workman?"

"Yeah well, things are already changing from our original plan. Remember? We were going to keep from getting together. It will be three months since we did the dirty deed and here we are haggling over what we should do about some woman we know nothing about."

"Look Bart, we're not haggling. We're discussing a possible problem just like anyone would. You've got to admit we have a problem. And like all bumps, we have to decide whether to navigate around them or plow through them. Let's not make this thing bigger than it is. First, we'll talk to the woman and go from there. OK? And Bart, nobody said anything about eliminating Mrs. Workman, - - nobody except you!

"Ah come on George. I know you better than that. The idea is hanging around, just below the surface. Don't try to bullshit a Guinea like me. We can't throw everyone that worries us out of a plane in the middle of the Cascade Mountains."

George started laughing. "Bart you sure have an imagination. I wasn't thinking that at all."

"Don't play games with me. This is serious shit. OK, I'll go and talk to this woman and see what we can do. By the way, have you heard anything about Brian Douglas?"

"I take the Seattle Times and check it everyday. So far nothing. The Wenatchee World hasn't reported anything either."

"I think that's pretty crazy. It seems like someone would be missing a man who won a multi-million dollar lottery. Don't the papers usually follow lottery winners for a few months? It just doesn't seem right."

"Frankly Bart, I'm glad we haven't heard anything. And why would we? You said it yourself. No man could survive the fall, and even he did, you saw those mountains all covered with snow. He would freeze to death. We didn't exactly leave him with a survival kit."

"What I meant George is that no one around Chelan has said anything and he lived here. You would think someone would call the Wenatchee World and ask about Brian Douglas. Where would you be if you had won all that money? Maybe you would go on a trip to some exotic place; Hawaii, Indonesia, Italy, France or Tahiti. He could be almost anywhere he wants to be, even at home. Life goes on for everyone else. Everyone has a life. He could be on his way to the moon."

George laughed heartily, "Lighten up my friend. Don't make up scenarios that aren't there."

"Yeah, well I hope you're right. George, would you do me a favor? Snoop around on Brian Douglas to see what's happening on that end?"

"Sure. I can't for a few days, but next week I'll have the time."

CHAPTER FOUR

Father Damon O'Reilly locked the front door of St. Joseph's Catholic Church and walked up the center aisle, half genuflected at the altar and headed to the rectory.

Where was Brian Douglas? It was unlike him to leave without saying something. He sat on the stool and tried to decide what do with the things Brian had left in the basement. Brian had gone out of his way to make room for the sole purpose of storing something important. Father O'Reilly was reminiscing about Brian's early life, when he got to know him and his family. It was as an altar boy he first met him. He was always quiet, almost shy, polite, but very attentive. He was close to his parents, especially his mother. Brian had gone to the local university and become an engineer, disappeared for twenty years and then came home again. He went back to working with his hands and became a carpenter, Brian had always loved building things and savored the finished product. He had dated a local girl that came to St. Joseph's church, but she had gone off to a different university and married someone else. After his father died, he took care of his mother until she passed on. He became somewhat reclusive, but always managed to stay in contact with the priest. They were good friends and would occasionally dine out together.

The knock on the front door of the church jolted Father O'Reilly from his introspection and he shuffled off to the entrance. He opened the door to see a woman, a short distance away, about to get into her car.

"Hello," Father O'Reilly yelled.

The woman turned, and approached the priest.

"Are you Father O'Reilly?"

"I am."

"I'm sorry…I hope I didn't distract you from something important. I'm, I'm embarrassed…I don't know what to say now that I'm here. I think I should go," she stammered and turned away.

"Please, stay. I assure you I won't bite. Come inside."

"I'm not a Catholic."

"You don't have to be. We're just going to talk. Please come in."

The woman followed Father O'Reilly into the church and they sat in the last pew.

She looked around the inside of the church, taking in the artwork and appointments.

"Catholic churches have always fascinated me, Father O'Reilly. They're so beautiful and reverent. Is that the right word? Have you ever been in St. Patrick's in New York City? I'm sorry. I really haven't been in that many, but the ones I have seen are so beautiful it almost makes me want to be a Catholic. I'm blithering because I'm nervous."

She averted her eyes, took a deep breath and looked back into his. "I have a friend by the name of Brian Douglas and he mentioned your name. Actually, he talks a lot about you. I guess you're good friends?"

"I'm delighted that he would consider me a good friend Ms...."

"Ooops, forgive me, I'm Christina Palmer," she laughed nervously.

"Ms. Palmer, I know Brian pretty well, and yes, we are good friends. I've known the man for most of his life."

"I guess he hasn't mentioned my name to you then, Father. Should I be calling you Father?"

"Now it's my turn to ooops. Please call me Damon."

"I like that; it kind of sounds biblical. I don't mind calling you Father but it sounds a little presumptuous since I'm not Catholic."

"I'm sure I've been called worse, and Damon is fine with me," Father O'Reilly responded amiably.

"Well Damon, you're the only person I knew to contact. I haven't heard from nor seen Brian in several months. I thought maybe I had said or done something that upset him."

"I too, have been wondering what happened to my friend. By coincidence he was on my mind when you knocked on the door. It's like he's disappeared into thin air."

"You don't suppose something bad happened to him, do you?"

Father O'Reilly shook his head. "I've racked my brain trying to remember our last conversations and nothing has jumped out at me. I can't come up with anything that would give any indication he was in trouble, or was bothering him. In fact, of late he has been on top of the world. It's a complete mystery. How long did you say you had known Brian?"

"Around five months. We met at the local fitness center and became fast friends. After I discovered he was a carpenter I asked him if he would consider doing my kitchen. Now I haven't seen him for so long that I thought it might have been something I said."

"I don't think it's anything you did or said. I feel like it might be more ominous."

"I don't quite understand," Christina replied.

"Well, recently his life took a turn that for most people would be a good omen, however, now I'm not so sure it was a good thing for him. Did he tell you anything that most people would consider good news?"

"I'm sorry Damon I can't think where you're going with this. Brian is so down to earth and…"

"What kind of work do you do Ms. Palmer?"

"I'm a teacher at the local high school."

"Are you and Brian in some kind of relationship?"

Her cheeks flushed and her eyes fell to the floor, "I'm sorry, I think I should be going," she mumbled as she stood.

"Please sit down Ms. Palmer," Damon pled quietly, "that was an unfair question. I was out of line. Please. My intention was to find out how much I should tell you."

Christina timidly resumed her seat, she took a deep breath and spoke quietly. "I think you could say we are very close friends, I like him very much and I thought he liked me."

"Then I can speculate with you what I think might be going on. I am totally at a loss to guess what could have happened to him, but I have a feeling it wasn't good. Brian left something with me and made me promise not to touch it unless I knew for sure he would never be coming back. At this moment, I'm not sure of anything. Now you're here and I have someone I can talk to. It's like a prayer has been answered. What I'm about to tell you is extremely confidential. As far as I know, you are the only other person that will know this. Brian won a very large sum of money. I don't know the exact amount, but it must have been a lot."

"You mean like some million dollar lottery win?"

"Yes, I think so, and I don't think you want to know about it. I feel better knowing I have a confidante, but please believe me, we could be in grave danger."

"You think someone else found out and that's why he disappeared?"

"I can only speculate, Christina."

"Well Father, from what he told me, you were his best friend. Do you think he didn't tell me because it might put me in danger?"

"Knowing Brian like I did like I do, yes. Getting back to your question, yes I do think someone found out. The lottery officials were aware of his name, I knew, I firmly believed that no one else did. But someone locally must have found out, and that's why Brian is gone. Somehow I believe he's alive, but I have no proof, just a deep-seated feeling. I also believe you and I Christina, are the only people who know Brian is missing."

"He never mentioned any family to me. Should we go to the police?" she asked quietly.

"I considered doing that a couple of weeks ago. Brian was a quiet man, not a recluse by any means, but a very private person. He liked the idea that no one knew he had won a lot of money. Informing anyone in authority would definitely open Pandora's box, don't you think?"

"I suppose you're right. Now that we've talked, I realize I didn't know Brian very well. I sensed he was a private person.

That might have been part of what I liked about him," Christina lamented.

CHAPTER FIVE

Bart Colangelo was about a mile from Chelan. As he drove from Wenatchee he thought about what he would say to Mrs. Workman. He knew he had to work something out with Tom's mother. George, bastard that he was, would be considering getting rid of her if he couldn't come up with something. He reached the crest of the hill and was looked down at a small portion of the fifty-mile long, beautiful blue basin. He had always liked the lake. It was one of the many reasons he had moved to the Wenatchee Valley. You could fish, boat, water ski, sail and swim in, the serene glassy water. There were small parks where one could barbeque and picnic. Bart drove over the bridge and through the town. He drove up a small hill and turned to the right, then checked the address he had written on a card.

The door opened after he had knocked twice.

"Are you the man that called?" the woman asked suspiciously.

"Yes, I'm Bart Colangelo," I said and waited for her to invite me in.

"What do know about Tom?"

"Mrs. Workman would it be possible to talk to you inside?"

After a moment of silence, she slowly opened the door and I walked into the front room.

"Sit down Mr. Angelo," she motioned to the sofa, then sat down across from me. "I'm sorry, but I'm concerned about Tom. I know something is very wrong. I just know it," she choked out through her tears.

"How long has he been missing, Mrs. Workman?"

She blew her nose, stood, and walked into the kitchen. A few minutes later she came back.

"Tom is not a lot of things that he should be, but the one thing he is…is dependable. This is not Tom. He wouldn't miss work and he wouldn't stay away for over three months. I haven't heard a word. That's just not Tom. I know something bad has happened to him," she sobbed. "I talked to the police and they couldn't tell me anything. Vandy told me that you knew Tom and I was hoping you could tell me something. Anything! Were you friends?"

I felt like hell. The crying and all was getting to me and I didn't want to lie to her. "Vandy was right, I knew Tom from playing softball on one of town teams. It sounds like you did all the right things in looking for him." I wanted to stop here and not go on lying but I felt like I had to say something that would make the poor woman feel better.

"How are you doing, Mrs. Workman?"

"I guess you know he lives here with me, and I do count on his help with the bills and all. We have some saved, but I will eventually have to take on a renter or something, if he doesn't come home," she whimpered.

I really did feel sorry for Mrs. Workman and that bothered me. She stood and walked away to another room. She was a nice looking woman, around my age, I thought, *but I was never very good at guessing ages. She came back into the front room looking more in control.*

"The problem is, because we don't know if he's dead or alive so I can't get his life insurance policy to pay. Someone has to declare him dead, God forbid, but I just don't know anything," she lamented.

"Mrs. Workman, I'll get together with some of the guys that know Tom and see if we can help out somehow, OK? And my name is Bart Colangelo."

"Isn't that what I called you?" she asked, "Colangelo, right?"

"Yes ma'am, that's right."

She smiled wanly and stood, "Thank you, Mr. Colangelo. I think I feel a little better now, - - not a lot, but a little," she smiled sadly.

I returned her weak smile and left. I really felt like hell. I hated the phony shit, and here I was - - knee deep in it."

"Hey Bart, how'd it go?" George greeted. "What's with the long face?"

"How did what go, George? What are you talking about?"

"Tom Workman's mother?"

"Yeah, well I feel sorry for her."

"So you do have a long face about it."

"Look George, I realize it was a freak accident. I just had to talk to a grieving woman who depended on him. She's going to have a hard time of it now. The mother has a life insurance policy on him but she can't collect on it because there's no body. It's a crummy situation, George."

"Well, I guess you could give her your share of the money we have Bart," George said sarcastically.

Bart looked hard at him with malice in his eyes. "It was an unfortunate accident that Tom Workman fell out of your plane, something none us had a hand in doing, but we shouldn't be celebrating his demise. I still have feelings even if you don't, you asshole."

George locked eyes with Bart and thought about going to blows with the slightly shorter man. But he knew Bart would kick his ass if he did. George wasn't afraid of Bart, but he knew Bart could be a bad ass in a fight and he was fearless. George broke the stare with a smile.

"Maybe we could cut Mrs. Workman in on some of the money. How much do you think we should give her Bart?"

"I don't think that's a good idea. I think we should look into how much life insurance Tom Workman had and consider giving her that amount, if it isn't too much."

"Did you quote her an amount?"

"No. I said I would talk to some of the guys that knew Tom. No amount was mentioned."

"I told her you were rich, George," and Bart laughed. George grinned.

"That's a horseshit lie Bart. You didn't tell her that."

"No I didn't. But if she asks, I will tell her that you are wealthy and very generous."

George Tilden was wealthy. He was a legitimate millionaire in the building contractor business. He has a good reputation in and around Douglas County and some of the connecting counties. I had always respected George Tilden. He was a smart businessman and knew how to work people, but I often wondered if he had a heart or soul. George knew people well. He could, in a short period of time analyze and know what to say and do to make that person do his bidding; a rare talent. Not that he did this to all the people he met, just those he chose. There were times I thought George had a heart, and then he would do or say something that nullified that thought. Was Ted Bundy totally bad? Did he ever help an old lady across the street? Was he kind to animals? Did he have long lasting friends?

The first time I was aware that George Tilden did things for people was when I read he gave the Mission, turkeys and food at Thanksgiving time and then again at Christmas.

I looked up to see George smiling at me.

"Were you able to find out anything about Brian Douglas?" I asked.

"Not really. No more than what we had known about the man when we chose to lighten him of some of his millions." George responded nonchalantly. "One of his neighbors said he was a good carpenter and that he was a loner. The lady thought his best friend was a priest at the Catholic Church. I guess Brian was pretty good with an acoustic guitar and so was the priest. She said she often heard the two playing music, said it was pretty good too. The neighbor also said that Brian had been seen with a woman on occasions, maybe a girlfriend."

"Did the neighbor say anything about his absence?"

"Just that it was a mystery. No explanation."

"What about family or extended family, relatives, old acquaintances?"

George shook his head.

"Are you going to talk to the priest or the woman?" Bart asked quietly.

"Yes I am Bart. I would have done it the same day but something came up with the business and I had to cut it short. The priest's name is father Damon O'Reilly. I figured he might know the woman Douglas has been seen with. This has really gotten under your skin."

"Hey George, the littlest mistake can lead to a lot trouble. I'm just trying to nip anything that will tie us to Brian, of the bud. Can't be too careful if we want to stay out of prison and enjoy some of the money. Wouldn't you agree?"

"I had forgotten what a great detail man you are Bart; one of your many strong points."

Two days later.

Father Damon O'Reilly opened the door to a man whose picture he had seen in the local paper.

"Father O'Reilly?" the man asked.

"Yes, I'm Father O'Reilly."

"My name is George Tilden. I understand you knew Brian Douglas."

"Yes, yes would you like to come in? My first name is Damon Mr. Tilden."

"Thank you Damon, I was wondering if I should call you father or your surname. I'm not Catholic."

"I gathered that Mr. Tilden."

George smiled at the priest. *This man is quite perceptive*, he thought.

"Would you like a cup of coffee Mr. Tilden?"

"No Thank you, Damon, I just finished lunch. I've always been curious. Do priests own homes, like this one?"

Damon smiled at the question. "No we don't. We take an oath of poverty. We don't own anything. People donate the cars we drive and the homes we live in. Are you considering becoming a priest, Mr. Tilden?"

"I can see you have a good sense of humor Damon. No, it was something I have always wanted to ask a priest…just curiosity."

"How well do you know Brian, Mr. Tilden?"

"Not well. I had a chance to talk to him about a home a year ago and now I can't seem to contact him."

"Brian wanted to buy a home from you?" Damon asked curiously.

George felt like he had said the wrong thing. "Not exactly. How well *did* you know Brian Douglas, Damon?"

Father O'Reilly paused at the question

" I gave his mother and father last rites. I think I know Brian about as well as anyone around this town. I can't imagine why he would have spoken to you about another house. You realize he already owns one."

What was I hearing in those words? George wondered. *I felt like the good priest was interrogating me.* "I'm sorry Damon, I'm not sure I understand your question."

"Why would Brian want to buy another house? He's alone and the need for another house seems strange to me, unless hewas contemplating a rental for extra income."

Now it was George Tilden's turn to wonder about Damon's question. "Well Damon, I didn't say he wanted to buy another house." What I said, was that I had a chance to talk to Brian about a house that I wanted to fix up and thought he might be interested in the job."

The priest nodded. "I think I understand Mr. Tilden. I apologize. I haven't heard from Brian for a while and his disappearance is starting to get to me. He's a journeyman carpenter and you would have gotten the best. He's done some work around the church and rectory."

This is what George was looking for now. The priest didn't know where Brian Douglas was and would probably never know. "Well Damon if you hear from him, would you give him my card and have him call?"

Father prayed at the altar after George Tilden left. He was confused. What could he do now? Maybe he should go to the authorities. What could the police do? Is it possible that what he had heard was true? He could have meant to say 'do' instead of 'did.' It was easy to say one by accident and mean the other. But Father O'Reilly, in the context of the conversation, had felt otherwise. But then why would Mr. Tilden come and ask questions about what he already knew.

And what did Father O'Reilly really know about Brian Douglas? There were years when Brian disappeared from the small town for several years and even his parents didn't know his whereabouts. 'Government work' was the answer given by his father and mother. He knew Brian to be quiet, yet not reclusive like one of his neighbors had described him. Brian had never asked him any personal questions and he had returned the courtesy.

Yes, we are a lot alike.

I wanted to do something. I was feeling helpless, and in need of communication with someone I could trust. Right now I was blank. Who do I trust implicitly?

I trekked home solemnly.

CHAPTER SIX

Brian Douglas had been watching Tom Wah Gee in awe as he practiced his disciplines. The man was big and yet, nimble as a ballet dancer. Brian was sure the man was at least in his mid fifties and yet sculptured like a Navy Seal. Gee ate very little, but still remained amply muscled from Yoga and the Shuai Chiao, the disciplines his uncle had said he practiced.

I stood and walked unsteadily outside. I still had a limp and my vision wasn't quite right yet; double vision and some blurriness, but I was mending as well as I could. I became brave enough to emulate my host's disciplines. Tom Wah Gee had been proud to have a rookie disciple and demonstrated great patience with me. Gee would mime the moves and then demonstrate each motion until I was able to imitate them. He would bow his approval and redo the ones he didn't approve of. He allowed very little error, even though my legs were not at one hundred percent. In fact, my whole body was not yet ready for the stringent discipline that he employed, but I didn't complain. We never spoke, and after a few months I began liking not talking. Somehow, not talking was a good thing. Things could be explained with gestures, body movements, and facial frowns or smiles. It really worked. Tom Wah Gee was a good teacher.

Needless to say I was shocked when Son Lo Gee arrived one day at his uncle's front door, big as life. Tom Gee had gone on some excursion and I was the reception committee.

"I'm Son Lo Gee, Tom Wah Gee's nephew and the person who wrote the note a few months ago. You did get the opportunity to read the small transcript I wrote, didn't you?" He asked as he eyeballed me up and down.

"Yes," I replied awkwardly.

"You were very lucky to be alive. You realize that you must have fallen or been pushed out of a low flying aircraft, don't you? Thank goodness for you the weather was bad on that day and the plane was forced to fly just above the treetops.

"Yes," I nodded.

"You're very lucky to be alive. If my uncle had not witnessed the actual falling and rescued you from the snow, I wouldn't be talking to you today."

All I could do was nod.

"I know my uncle doesn't keep any kind of mirrors in his cabin, so you're probably not aware of your physical appearance?"

I touched my now hairy face.

"Yes, your face took a lot of the abuse from the fall. At some point you're going to require an abundance of plastic surgery and maybe some orthopedic reconstruction." How are your legs doing? Without taking x-rays of your ribcage, I believe you have some fractured and broken ribs. I can see your left arm will require some reconstruction too. Essentially, you're a mess right now Mr." The doctor looked squarely into my eyes. I see you have some partial blindness in your right eye, probably some in the other eye Mr."

"Brian…

"Mr. Brian."

I smiled at the good doctor.

"I'm happy to see you keep a positive outlook, Mr. Brian. I'm sure you will need some psychological testing for this horrific trauma you've been through. All in good time. Is my uncle around?"

"He should be here soon, Doctor Gee."

"I don't know anything about you Mr. Brian. We didn't find any identification on you when my uncle dragged you here."

At first, when I woke up, I didn't know who I was, but now that you've brought it up, some of my memory has come back. I realize my name is Brian Douglas."

"Oh, your name is Brian Douglas?"

"Yes sir, I didn't want to correct you earlier because…yes, Brian Douglas."

"And do you know if you fell out of the plane or was it something more sinister," the doctor asked earnestly.

"I believe it was the latter. I had never seen any of the men that did this to me before."

"Are you in some kind of trouble with these men? It seems to me like getting tossed out of an airplane is quite serious, wouldn't you agree?"

I smiled. "Most definitely, Dr. Gee. The notes you left with the explanation were excellent, sir. I don't know when I'll be able to walk out of this place. Maybe you could arrange for someone to move me to your facility. I assessed that I would need a good bone doctor, and you're right about my not seeing my face. But it sounds like your diagnosis of 'messed up,' pretty well sums it up. I assumed that I would be needing plastic surgery."

"I hate bringing this up but, how are your finances, Mr. Douglas?"

"I don't know how I know this or where it came from, but I have a large amount of money in a bank in Seattle. Let me put it this way, Dr. Gee. I could rent a helicopter to pick me up from here. But if you could arrange it for me, I'll pay for it. I will reimburse you for the treatment you gave when you found me. Would you be kind enough to find me the best plastic surgeon available?"

"Douglas, Douglas should I be familiar with your name?"

"Not really, and I'm happy about that. It is not my nature to boast as I just did. But I wanted you to know I can afford whatever it costs. The sooner I get out of here the sooner I can start my rehabilitation, no offense to your uncle. I have learned a great deal from this holy man. If I can be put back together in the next six months I can go back to my life with your help, Dr. Gee."

"I'll leave tomorrow and make all the arrangements. I brought you a special phone with a special battery that operates by solar power so we can communicate, Mr. Douglas."

"I will never be able to thank you and you uncle enough for what you have done for me, but I'll try, sir. By the way, how do you get in and out of this place?"

"I hike for twenty three point nine miles until I reach a dirt road that takes me to a paved road that takes me to highway 97. Depending on the weather, it takes me about thirty-six hours to reach the dirt road where my Jeep takes me the rest of the way. I only do this once a year. I'm a hobby hiker to begin with, so it has a dual effect." The uncle arrived just then and he and Dr. Gee walked outside.

I picked up my cell phone and started making some calls. Doctor Gee is an extremely detailed man, I thought. The cell phone was pure genius. I didn't even know they had such a thing as a solar cell battery.

Wow. I now liked Yoga and would integrate it into my life. I was feeling good. This whole nightmare had changed me. I wasn't sure how, but I felt like it would be for the good. Mentally I was on a high. The two men finally came inside. The uncle went into his room and doctor began putting some food together.

"I made some calls to my bank and located a helicopter agency. If you like, Dr. Gee, the copter can pick you up tomorrow at four PM.

"You've been a busy bee, Mr. Douglas."

"The magic of the phone you brought me," I said holding it up.

Dr. Gee nodded. "Four o'clock would be fine. I can see you're a man of action."

I thought about his statement. Was I a man of action? At the moment, I wasn't sure what kind of man I was. I knew I had a lot of money, but I wasn't sure from where yet. About all I was sure of was that I hadn't stolen it, and I wasn't one hundred percent sure about that.

CHAPTER SEVEN

Christina Palmer had driven over to Father O'Reilly's residence last Tuesday but got cold feet and left. Today she was determined to talk to the priest. The idea that no one was doing anything about the disappearance of Brian Douglas was just too much for her to bear. She wasn't able to sleep well at night and wasn't eating well. Her mind was running wild with reasons he was not around. Even now she found herself standing on the doorstep to the priest's home, unaware she had left her car. Stress, she thought. She rang the doorbell.

"Yes," a short lady responded at the open door.

"I, I would like to speak to the priest."

"Father O'Reilly or...

"Yes Father O'Reilly, I interrupted.

"Hi Christina," the priest greeted me from behind the lady, "I'll take it from here Mrs. Langston, this is Christina Palmer, a friend of mine." He spoke softly to Mrs. Langston and she left.

"Would you like to come in Christina?"

"Would you mind if we walked," she requested.

"Why yes. It's a pretty day. A walk would be good."

The church was a short way from the park that bordered Lake Chelan. The pristine waterway was fifty miles long. They walked talking about the beauty of the surroundings, into the well-kept park. It was a weekday so the park was dotted with mostly retired people, and not many of them.

"Would you like to sit at one of the park benches, Christina?"

She nodded and they sat.

"Down deep I feel that something bad has happened to Brian," Christina lamented.

"With regret, I share your feelings."

"It has been too long. I just can't believe that one of us hasn't heard from him, and it's starting to affect my health. I'm at a dead end. I was hoping you might have something, anything, Damon."

"I've thought about going to the local police and at least notifying them that he's is missing. The problem is, I'm not a blood relative. The police department has rules about what they can do and not do, even if I were a blood relative. Brian once mentioned he had an uncle on his mother's side that lived back east, but that's all I know about that. I don't even know what state the man lives in. I just don't have enough to go to the authorities. There is something that has been festering in me for over two weeks now. At that time, I wanted very much to talk to someone about it. I don't know anyone well enough to confide something that isn't concrete. At this moment it seems absurd to even mention it."

We sat quietly; Christina staring out at the beautiful lake, but seeing nothing and me in bleak doubt.

"Damon would you tell me what was festering in you?"

"A Mr. Tilden came to see me a couple of weeks ago. Said he'd talked to Brian months earlier, but couldn't locate him lately. Mr. Tilden develops home and commercial property. Anyway, he said that the reason he had talked to Brian was to hire him to rebuild a kitchen in one of his homes. Knew that Brian was a top journeyman in carpentry, honest, reliable and that he had been available at that time. Someone had referred Mr. Tilden to me when he was inquiring about hiring Brian for another more current job. These are his exact words, Christina. "How well *did* you know Brian Douglas?"

Christina looked directly into Damon's eyes. "*Did* instead of *do*? And you think it might have been a Freudian slip by Mr. Tilden."

"I do. I didn't correct him and I believe he wasn't aware of what he had said or he was smug enough to think I didn't catch the slip. You see when he first talked to me about Brian, Tilden said he had talked to him about a house. I questioned him about that and he changed it to fixing up a house."

"You lost me, Damon."

"Well, I'm not sure I know what I'm trying to say. But what I think I'm alluding to is that Mr. Tilden was on fishing trip with me."

Christina looked at me with complete confusion on her face.

Mr. Tilden wanted to know what I knew about Brian. I know I'm reaching, but at the time, that is what I thought."

"And now?"

"I don't know. It's all hazy, convoluted and very confusing. I keep grasping at straws. Maybe everything Mr. Tilden said was straight and true and it's me that's doing the making up."

"Damon, I don't think you're grasping at straws. You're just aware, like myself; that something is wrong and you're looking for answers. Your reasoning is acute to every bit of information. I think I understand. We feel like we're under pressure to find some answers."

Damon nodded.

"I think one of us should go to the police and report Brian's disappearance. We probably should have done it months ago. I'm here today because I feel like you've known him longer than I, but I can't wait any longer. We need answers, so we've got to start asking questions to those in authority. Right now, no one is doing anything and that's worse. We have to do something, even if it's wrong. You and I need to become detectives and do our own investigation. If we want something to happen, we're going to have do it ourselves."

"Christina, I'm on your side. What do you want me to do?" Damon asked eagerly.

"Would you mind going back to where Mr.Tilden got your name from that neighbor and talk to him or anybody else that knows any tidbit about Brian and I'll hit the police department. I want to know what they will do and what they can't do."

The two discussed their strategy and decided to meet the following Tuesday.

Christina Palmer had been reluctant to approach Brian's house. She knew Brian well enough to pick up the paper, if he took one, but she felt like it was too much intrusion. Brian had conveyed that independence, that seclusion, but she had driven by his house. It looked neglected, down trodden and lonely. She felt sad as she drove by on her way to police station. As she approached the Information Desk she hesitated and was suddenly compelled to turn and leave.

"Can I help you with something ma'am," the desk officer offered.

"Yes, I believe you can. I want to report a missing person."

"Would this be a family member?"

"No, just a good friend."

"What is your friend's name and address?"

"Brian Douglas, and he lives at 967 Entiat Street, Chelan.

"What makes you think this person is missing?"

"It's been a little over four months since I've seen or heard from him, which is very unusual."

"What about family members. Have you made contact with any of them?"

"I don't think he has any family living here."

"What about neighbors?"

"Well, I have a friend, Father O'Reilly, that is going to do some investigating with the neighbors."

"I think we could send someone out to check with the neighbors and then, if we don't get any answers we could do a welfare check on the man. This Father O'Reilly. Is that his surname or is he a Catholic priest?"

I smiled. "He's a Catholic priest."

"Could I have your name and telephone number?"

I gave the officer my name and telephone number.

"Ms. Palmer, this will take a couple of days to get started. If you hear from this man between now and then, would you call us and let us know. Here's the number you can call. He might be in Hawaii, or the Greek Islands or on some four month hiatus, having a ball."

I rolled my eyes and checked the card he gave me, "Somehow I don't think so officer Landis."

The following Tuesday:

"Thanks for meeting me here at the park, Christina.

She nodded. "Were you able to talk to any of Brian's neighbors?"

"That would be great Damon. Were you able to talk to any of Brian's neighbors?"

"Yes, and the neighbor across the street had been aware that Brian hadn't been around. Mrs. Latham told me that it wasn't too unusual because Brian had worked for the FBI or CIA, some government job, a few years ago and just thought they might have called him back for some reason."

"Were you aware he had held a government job Damon?" Chris asked.

He shook his head. "No. No I wasn't. I'm not the kind of guy that wants to know things; especially about someone like Brian. If he wanted to tell me something I would gladly listen, but I wouldn't try to illicit information from the man. Without saying it, his body and facial language told me that. I respected that in him, that's all."

"Your absolutely right, Damon. I received the same impression from him. Damon nodded. "Without saying anything he could make you feel like a special friend."

They sat quietly for a few seconds contemplating each other's words.

"I did manage to talk to a lone neighbor, Mrs. Dill, up the block who mentioned Brian might have known the mailman," Damon finally said. "She thinks the letter carriers first name was Tom, didn't know his last name. They don't carry name tags on their uniforms, she had informed me."

"Well, now we're getting somewhere. The mailman's name is Tom. Let's see now Damon. How would knowing the mailman's name be a good thing?" She inquired.

"Well, don't we all have to inform the mail carriers if we're going to be gone for a few weeks or months."

"That's right, Damon. Did you ever walk up to Brian's front door and noticethe mailbox?"

"No. I never did. Did you?"

Chris thought about that for a second. "No, but guess what? His mail drop was in the garage door. One time I had to get some measurements for a cabinet to him and he told me to drop them off at the garage door letter slot. I don't think he took the local paper either. I've driven by his house but never noticed anything unusual, and now I know why. Hey Damon, we're starting to get somewhere. I mean, we're doing something and I'm feeling good from it. Aren't you?"

" Chris. Can I call you Chris?"

"Most people do."

"I wish I had known you were as worried as I've been and we might have gotten things going earlier, but at least we're doing it now. The other thing I found strange is that people don't know their neighbors. Two of the neighbors didn't even know the Douglas's lived in that small house in the middle of the block."

"I'm really not surprised. I did go to the police department and submitted a missing person report on Brian. There's a two-day waiting period before they'll start. A detective will be given the task of investigating, essentially what you're doing now, Damon and they'll check out his residence too."

Christina Palmer, dressed in gray sweats, her hair pulled back a slick, black ponytail, sat in the kitchen lacing up her jogging shoes, nearly ready to go for her Saturday morning run, when the phone rang.

Ms. Palmer. This is Detective Harris.

Christina immediately recognized her voice. "Yes," she said, did you find Brian?"

There was a pause. "Not yet. But I may have turned up something interesting. Can you meet me at his residence?"

Feeling a rush of excitement, Christina didn't hesitate, "I can be there in twenty minutes." She set the phone back down in its cradle. Her hand trembled in apprehension. What of it wasn't good news? she thought. What if...no? she stopped. You mustn't let the negativity creep into your thinking, she told herself.

Then thumbing through her address book, she picked up the phone. When Father O'Reilly came on the line, she filled him in on Harris's call and asked if he would accompany her to the meeting with the detective.

"What did she discover?" he asked.

"I don't know. She wouldn't say on the phone." She tapped fingernails on the tiled kitchen counter. "Can you make it then?"

"Well," he said," I'm almost finished with the final draft of my Sunday sermon...so I suppose..."

"Oh thank you," Christina interrupted, "I'll pick you up in fifteen minutes." Hanging up the phone, she grabbed her car keys and gym bag, and hurried out the door to her car.

Twenty-two minutes later, under a lead-gray sky, Christina veered the Honda to a stop in front of Brian Douglas's home. She and Father O'Reilly climbed out. She took the lead, taking long strides up the sloping drive, past the police cruiser parked in the driveway; Father hurried along behind.

Christina was about to take the wooden porch steps up to the front door when she heard the detective's voice say, "over here."

Detective Harris appeared from around the corner of the house.

Christina couldn't keep the emotion out of her voice. "What did you find?"

The detective pulled her notepad from inside her suit pocket and flipped the pages. "Let's go inside."

Harris led Christina and Father O'Reilly into the modest home. Inside the air felt close and musty. The furniture, much of it appeared to be handmade, had a patina of dust.

"He liked everything in its place all right, Father O'Reilly volunteered as they walked out of the house.

Christina nodded.

"Do you know if he had any enemies?" Harris asked.

They shook their heads.

"What about mail?" Chris asked.

The detective turned, "Oops, I forgot the garage." She went inside the house and we heard the automatic garage door opening. The two walked over to the open garage door and saw all of four months worth of scattered mail lying on the concrete floor.

"There's more, but I collected some this morning when I first arrived and placed it on his desk, inside. I took the liberty of opening a couple of letters from the Justice Department. Were either of you aware that Mr. Douglas had worked for ATF."

Again they both shook their heads.

"What is the ATF," Chris asked.

"It's the part of the government that handles, Alcohol, Tobacco, Firearms, and now also Explosives, under the jurisdiction of The Justice Department. Anyhow there is enough in these letters to indicate that Mr. Douglas worked for the Justice Department and more specifically for the ATF," Detective Burris informed them.

She pointed to the mail on the concrete floor. "I'm guessing his mail won't tell us where Mr. Douglas is, but his house indicates he was not abducted from here by force. Wouldn't you agree?"

The two agreed in unison, "yes."

"What did you think Brian did for a living, Damon?"

"Well, I knew for a fact that he was a smart, well educated man. I thought he had worked in some professional job as an engineer of some sort. For sure I was surprised to hear you say he had worked for ATF. I also knew that his hobbies were carpentry and music. He labored professionally as a carpenter for the last six or seven years."

"And you stated in your missing person report that he was a carpenter. Right Ms. Palmer?"

"Yes, but why do you think us knowing that Brian worked for the Justice department wouldn't help us find him."

"I think I said, I didn't think it would. Well because he mustered out of the justice job after retiring and he's been around here for almost six years.

The man recently turned fifty and I thought his previous job was, too much in the past, however, it might help. In fact I'll make my priority to check out his past with AFT, and see where that takes us. I'm the only detective allocated to this case, so I'm going to ask my boss if I can use your assistance. Is that OK?"

Damon glanced over at Chris and she was nodding. "We'd be glad to help out, Detective Harris. We both feel that doing something makes us better. The little we have already done has raised our spirits, for sure."

"Good. Now at some point I may stop any inquires if I think it may bring danger to you. We don't want your lives endangered in any way. Can we agree on that?"

They both nodded.

"All right Damon, Chris I have a lot of paper work to do on our friend Brian Douglas. Do either of you have anything else to report before we break up here?"

Damon raised his hand. "Ah, yes. Two things. One of the neighbors did mention that Brian had worked for the government. Do you think I should go back and talk to her?"

The detective nodded, "Yes. Find out how she knew that and anything else she might know. What was the other thing?"

"I'm not sure if this means anything but I talked to a commercial and residential building contractor recently about Brian." I paused. Well it wasn't important. I apologize. I'll keep knocking on doors detective."

"All right Damon, Chris. Do you mind if we meet at the police department the next time; they have a nice conference room. Damon are you available on Thursdays around four?"

He nodded.

"What about you Chris. I know you're a teacher, would that be cutting close for you?"

"I think that will be all right, detective."

"Good. Call me at the number I gave you if you can't make it. See you then. Keep good notes."

Damon and Chris walked to her car. "I think you should have told her what you thought about Mr. Tilden, Damon."

"Yes, I suppose I should have. I have it down in my notes, so at the next meeting I will. I like the detective. She's just regular people, don't you think?

"Yes, she is. I was surprised that she wanted our help."

"Maybe it's because the department is small, and we're just doing some of the grunt work, Chris."

"I was wondering if I could come along with you when you talk to the neighbor that said Brian had worked for the government."

"What about school"

"We're through for the summer next Monday."

"Sure Chris, I'd be glad to have you along."

CHAPTER EIGHT

Brian Douglas woke up. His eyelids didn't want to open and when they did, his eyes wouldn't focus. There was a very blurred face looking down at him.

"Mr. Douglas. Are you having trouble focusing?"

"Where am I?" he asked.

"St Jude's Hospital," the nurse responded as she hurried out of the room.

What am I doing in a hospital? Mr. Douglas? Is that what she called me?

"Good you're awake Mr. Douglas. The nurse thinks you might be having trouble with your vision. Is that correct?"

"Yes, I can't focus on anything."

"The nurse is bringing me some special drops to put in your eyes."

"Why am I in a hospital sir?"

"I'm Dr. Benjimen Roske, Mr. Douglas. Do you remember talking to me two days ago? The drops are here and I'm going to put some in you eyes. You're going to feel some cold, don't be alarmed."

I did feel the drops as they hit my eyes. They made me blink several times and then the doctor's face began to come into view. "No I don't remember talking to you, sir."

"That's all right. We, you and I, had discussed this very possibility. It is temporary, and Dr. Gee, the man that first discovered you out in the Cascade Mountains says it's all connected to your fall from a plane. I assure you Mr. Douglas, you're in good hands and we're going to have you up and around in no time. Your memory, however, will be in and out for a while. That's going to need some work. We have someone that will help you after we get you up and around. Can I get you anything?"

"I can't seem to move my hands."

"We're running some meds through IV's to you and don't want you to pull them out so we have you handcuffed with cotton straps. Unfortunately, we're going to have to leave them on for your own good. Again it's a temporary measure, and we'll remove them the minute you're able to sit up and stand. OK? We have a urethral tube in you and if you have the need to urinate, just let it go. Do you have any questions? If you need anything that the nurse can't help you with, don't hesitate to call for me. I'm Dr. Roske."

24 hours later:
>I woke and looked up at a ceiling. I couldn't tell whether it was day or night. I could hardly move my head from side to side.
>"Is there anyone close by that can hear me?"
>A face appeared beside the bed. "What can I do for you, Mr. Douglas?"
>"I seemed to be tied down. I can't move my hands."
>"Mr. Douglas, I'm Dr. Angie Lansing. There is a reason for the restraints. You've had some special work on your face and we don't want you to undo all that hard work. Not that you would do that on purpose but that you might do it without realizing it. Once you're able to stand and walk we'll remove the restraints sir."
>"What happened to my face?"
"Well, that's a long story. About all I can say is that it required a lot of plastic surgery to bring your face back to what you looked like. Dr. Gee is more qualified to tell you about the accident you had.
>"I guess that means I'm in a hospital."
>"Yes, Mr. Douglas you're in Jude's Hospital, Seattle, Washington."
>"So I live in Seattle?"
>"That I don't know. We're not sure where you live Mr. Douglas. All we know is that you have an account with a Seattle bank. The bank will not give any more information because we are not relatives. You gave Dr. Gee your name, but that's about all we know about you. Even you were surprised to know you had this Seattle account; lucky for you. It's what got you out of

the Cascade Mountains and into this hospital. There is very little known about you sir and that's one of the reasons I have been brought into your rehabilitation."

I turned my eyes away from the doctor and felt like hell. Someone out there has to know me and where I live and what I do. I don't even know how I got into this mess. An accident? What accident?

"Was I in a car accident?" I asked.

"About all I can say about the accident is that you had fallen down a very snowy mountain side and the rough snow had acted as sandpaper on your exposed face, thereby requiring plastic surgery."

"Snowy sandpaper?"

"Mr. Douglas you're getting the best treatment available for your condition, I assure you. When we're through with you George Clooney would be envious." I could see his eyes were smiling. "All in good time sir, all in good time."

CHAPTER NINE

"Now I'm in deep shit," Vandy wailed.

Bart studied him for a few seconds. "I've talked to Mrs. Workman. Yes she is worried about Tom but its got nothing to do with us Vandy."

"Yes it does because I picked him up that day to go play softball."

"I understand that you feel responsible for his safety, but you're not his big brother. You picked him up and you both went to play softball and then you lost track of him at one of the diamonds. You don't know what happened to him anymore than his mother."

"I never thought of that. There are three softball diamonds up there and I lost contact with him. Yeah, okay, I guess I could always say that. What about the money that Tilden was going to give his mother?"

"We can't do that either Vandy."

"Why?"

"Because we don't know where he is. Think about it. If we gave his mother even one thousand dollars, she would wonder why. It's like we're admitting that Tom is never coming back and that somehow we feel responsible. Vandy if I disappeared tomorrow and I was missing for, let's say three months, would you want to donate some money to my mother, if I had one?"

Vandy looked hard at Bart. "No I guess I wouldn't."

"If Loretta Workman asks you about Tom again just tell her what we just said, OK. It was a good idea about giving money to Mrs. Workman and we would never miss it, but it could get us in trouble in the long run, capisce?"

"Have you already talked to Tilden about it?"

"No Vandy, I haven't, but I will. Try not to talk to Mrs. Workman. Don't try to avoid her, but don't go to her for anything. OK? Does she have your telephone number?"

"I don't know. I don't think she does, but Tom might have had it."

"How did she get a hold of you the last time?"

"Oh, I went to her because I had picked him up to go to the diamonds and I knew she would want to talk to me. That's about the same time some detective asked me about Tom."

Bart froze in his seat. "What detective?"

"Hey Bart don't go getting excited. That was about three months ago."

"So tell me about it."

"Not much to tell, I don't remember the detective's name but he came to the house. He wanted to know how long I had known Tom and about the day I picked him up to go play softball."

"What did you tell him?"

"Well, that I had picked him up and we arrived at diamonds and then we got separated and I never saw him the rest of the day. I didn't know how he got home. That's it."

"Do you think he bought it?"

"I haven't seen him since."

"Vandy why didn't you say something about this when it happened?"

"I was going to mention it when I saw you or Tilden, but I didn't see either one of you for almost two weeks. By then, I had forgotten it."

They ordered another beer.

"And you say that was three months ago?"

"Well it was probably closer to four months, give or take a week. By the way, I've been wanting to ask you and Tilden if you had heard anything about Douglas."

"Why would we hear anything about someone that took a dive into the middle of the Cascade Mountains in the middle of winter?"

"I don't know. Stranger things have happened."

"Like what?"

"I don't know Bart. I just wondered if you had heard anything, that's all."

"I haven't heard anything, and I don't think George has heard anything, and I don't think we will."

CHAPTER TEN

Chris Palmer and Father O'Reilly stopped in front of Mrs. Latham's house.

"Have you talked to the people in that house there," Chris pointed.

"No I haven't. Either they're not home when I knocked or they don't ever answer the door."

Damon knocked. "Oh, Father O'Reilly, nice to see you again, please come in. Have you found out anything new about Mr. Douglas?"

"Mrs. Latham, this is Christina Palmer. She's Brian's friend."

"Nice to meet you Christina. I think I've seen you over at Mr. Douglas's house. He didn't have a lot of friends, so I noticed the ones he did have." They shook hands went into the kitchen where they all sat down.

"Coffee anyone," Mrs. Latham asked.

They declined.

"Tell us about how you knew that Brian had worked for the government."

"Like I told you before, Father, I was good friends with Sara Douglas and she had mentioned that Brian worked for the government. I don't know what part of the government he worked for, and she never did say."

"When you say Sara, that was Brian's mother?"

"Yes."

"I believe it was you that said Brian knew Tom the mailman, not just as the guy that brought the mail, but as a friend."

"Well, Father, I'm not sure that they were buddies, but one time I saw them carry on a ten or fifteen minute conversation while Tom was working, over at Brian's house. I guess I sound like some meddling old lady."

"I don't think that for a second. You just had an interest in your neighbors."

"Father, did you know that Tom disappeared about the same time as Brian?"

"What makes you say that Mrs. Latham?" Chris asked.

"Honey, call me Heidi. Well, for one thing, Father quit coming around. You two, and she looked over at the priest, used to carry on, singing and playing your guitars. Plus about the same time the neighborhood got a new mailman. I remember thinking it was quite a coincidence that Brian was gone and so was Tom. It may not have been the same day, but I think it was the same week. Well, I've got a doctor's appointment in thirty-five minutes and I have to go. It was nice meeting you Chris, and I hope to see you again."

Heidi Latham walked to the door with them and stepped outside.

"I was just thinking that you two should talk to the Medici's on the corner." She pointed to the white house with brown trim. "They both have some theories about this whole thing."

"What was their name?" Chris asked.

"Lilly and Roger Medici, they're Italian you know. Yup, you should go talk to them. I think I see their car in the driveway right now. OK, I gotta go."

Thanks again Heidi.

"What do you think Damon?"

"Sure, let's go."

The walk was brief and in less than five minutes they were on the front porch of the Medici residence, knocking. A man looked out from a pulled back curtain; the door opened. "You two solicitors?" the man asked as he looked us over. "Oh, Father O'Reilly, I didn't recognize you without your collar. Come in. Lilly its Father O'Reilly and a lady," the man yelled as they stepped into the front room.

"Hi Father, we saw you walking up the street and thought you might be Jahovah Witness," Lilly greeted.

"I can understand that, Mrs. Medici. This is Christina Palmer."

"Happy to meet you Miss Palmer. What are you two up to? Lilly asked.

"We were talking to Heidi Latham about Brian Douglas and his disappearance and she thought we should talk to you about him and Tom the mailman."

Lilly looked over at Roger as they all were seated in the front room.

"Let me tell them what I think Lilly," Roger injected. "You know that those two birds disappeared at the same time. People think it's quite a coincidence. I don't. I think whoever did them in, did them in together. We know the day that the mailman left his job, because it was in the beginning of the week. On Monday he delivered the mail and that was the last day anyone saw the man. Now the reason I think that was the day that this Brian character vanished is because, you, Father, didn't show up to have your Tuesday recitals. That's according to Heidi Latham. Now, I can't tell you who or why, but that's my theories."

"Roger has nothing Father, Chris. They're just speculations," Lilly ventured rolling here eyes.

"What do you think happened to Brian, Roger," Chris asked seriously.

"Well, I don't know if you know this, but Brian Douglas worked for the government; maybe FBI or CIA or some other organization. Anyway, these guys make enemies and they meet a lot of under handed characters, you know, bad guys. There are a lot of Osama Bin Laden's people that are starting to pop up in this country. You know like that Al Qaeda guy in Texas who was a psychiatrist in the Army and killed all those soldiers. I think one of these groups had it in for Brian and Tom, the mailman just happened to be in the wrong place at the wrong time."

"That's an interesting theory Roger. It made me think about when I first missed Brian and I believe you're right about the day. We always met on Tuesday and I remember he didn't call, so we didn't meet. I've never been one to impose myself on anyone. Especially a good friend like Brian," Father lamented.

"I too, was a good friend to Brian," Chris spoke up, "and I had left him a message on his phone about some kitchen measurements that he needed and I never got a response. I believe that was on a Sunday, now that I think about it."

Everyone's eyes landed on Lilly. She shook her head. "I don't know what happened. Tom the mailman was here one day and then he disappeared. I have no idea what happened to Mr. Douglas.

"You know Chris, Roger Medici was on target about when Brian disappeared. I hadn't focused on the day he was gone, but he appears to be very close to the actual day. He had an interesting theory, but I don't think I could buy into it."

"Yes, he was right about the day, even though I could never prove it."

Thursday meeting:

Detective Marci Harris rushed into the conference room a few minutes late.

"I finally called the detective that opened the file on Tom Workman. That detective is now working up in Okanogan, Omak and Tonasket. Sorry I'm late. One of the problems all cities, state and some federal employees are facing is lay offs. Our department was already operating on a shoestring budget and now there are just two of us, when we should have a minimum of four detectives. There is no one to blame, and we have to do with what we have. I want you two to know, I really appreciate all the assistance you're giving me. I hope I don't get you in any trouble by doing this. My boss has given me all the leeway on this case. All right let's get this dog and pony show on the road."

Father O'Reilly and Christina Palmer looked at each other smiled and started applauding.

Chris Palmer spoke first. "Does that mean no one had reported Brian missing until February 7th when I reported him missing?"

"You got it girl." Harris opened a manila folder. "Tom workman's mother reported her son missing on Thursday 11/30/11 at 9:00 AM, and you reported Brian missing on

February 7th, 2012. Can I ask you two why you would wait so long to report your friend missing?"

"We wondered the same thing," Father O'Reilly said. "Part of it is the kind of person that Brian Douglas is and the other reason is the kind of people that Chris and I are. It's not quite an oxymoron for me to say that I'm a loner when I get up in front of a throng of people and speak every Sunday. One would think I love people, and I do, but I like my down time too. I think Chris is the same kind of person. I'd even go out on a thin limb to say that Brian Douglas is also a conservative person."

Christina nodded demurely.

"I think I understand. Well, from now on we're not letting time march on without us. We're going to find out where Brian Douglas has gone. Right at this moment Christina, do you think Brian Douglas is alive?"

"Yes, and I think I speak for Father O'Reilly too. We regret we did nothing for so long, but feel that he's alive and we're going to find him, with your help, of course, Detective Harris."

"Good, now I think I should go and talk to Mr. Tilden and any anyone that knew Mr. Workman, including his mother. Have either of you talked to Loretta Workman?"

Chris spoke up, "Until just recently, we didn't know that Tom Workman had known Brian. So we didn't have any reason to talk to the mailman."

"That's all right. I'll go and talk to her. Don't stop talking to the neighbors. Someone out there knows something. I'm running late for another meeting, but I'll see you next week. Keep up the good work."

Detective Harris was going over her notes in the conference room when her phone rang.

"Harris."

"I got your email. Come on over and we'll talk," her Lieutenant summoned.

Detective Harris liked Toby Moriarty, her boss and friend. He had been a detective in San Jose, California. She remembered when he had arrived five years ago. He and his wife had vacationed in Chelan, Washington and fell in love with the small sleepy retirement town and they had moved here. Toby and his wife had come to the Pacific Northwest for the ubiquitous evergreen trees, beautiful lake, the chill of cold in the winter, and the endless friendliness of the laid back sparse population. They could see real cherry, apple and apricot trees as well as almost any other type of fruit tree. They could even pick their own fruit right off the tree if they wished. They were able to smell the clean air and of course enjoy the seasonal changes. Toby Moriarty was also the first African American Detective in the little lakeside community, and the town loved the soft-spoken police detective. He and his wife had gladly left the crowds, the endless lines of traffic, the beeping horns, congestion at every corner, the endless concrete and asphalt landscape; the steady hum of cars on 101 and the late night trains carrying their goods to all of the California towns and cites that lie along a majestic Pacific Ocean.

"Please sit down, Harris."

"I would like to run something by you, Toby. I got the name of a prominent man in Wenatchee, who does a lot business here in Chelan, as well as in Cashmere, Leavenworth and some of the towns running up to the Canadian border. He's a commercial and residential builder. Anyway, I've never spoken to him and I wanted to know if I should make an appointment, or just go in cold."

"Well, if you make an appointment, he'll be ready for what he thinks you'll want to ask him. Is this about the Workman case?"

"Yes."

"What's the man's name?"

"George Tilden."

He nodded, "I've met him. He's smooth. Says all the right things and does a lot smiling. Carries a lot of clout in Wenatchee. I heard some things about him that aren't good, but I don't know if they're true, so I won't comment. When you step on toes like he has to get where he is, you make a lot people mad at you. On the other hand, if you just walk into his office, you might catch him off guard and he might say things he wouldn't say otherwise. The spontaneous approach might bring out the real man. But it *might* make you an enemy."

"Good, I was kind of thinking along those lines, but I wanted to see what you thought. I'll let what you said resonate for a while before I decide what I'm going to do." She stood.

"I'm sorry I was so long sitting on this thing Harris. In my estimation it wasn't a priority and we were short staffed even then. You were on the Martinez homicide and I was on the child care case."

"Yes, I remember Toby. Getting back to my case at hand. Do you think Workman and Douglas are dead?'

"You know Harris, ever since I put you on this case, it has baffled me. I was going over the notes you've given me and it's hard to believe that we haven't heard a word about the two and they're not even connected, I don't think. Right now I wouldn't give much hope that either one is alive. What do you think?"

"I really don't know, but I'm inclined to believe as you do. However, you know what's strange? The two citizens I have going door to door, know Brian Douglas and I asked them the same question. They both believe he's alive. They didn't speculate about it. Both said without hesitation that he was alive."

Toby scratched his head, "that's very interesting. Do you think either of them could be involved in some way?"

"Well, it would certainly be a blow to my ego if either was somehow involved. Father O'Reilly was a good friend to Brian Douglas and had known him since he was a young man, although he was surprised to find out that Brian had worked for ATF. Chris Palmer hadn't known Brian very long but I think they had a romantic thing going. They met when he did some carpenter work for her. I think she likes the guy. I have to admit they are a strange threesome Toby."

The Lieutenant's phone rang. "I'll catch you later Harris." She waved goodbye and exited his office.

CHAPTER ELEVEN

"Mr. Tilden, Detective Harris is here to see you sir."

"Who?"

"Detective Harris." What would a detective want with me? I donate to policeman's ball every year and the fireman's kid drive. "Send him in Rose."

"He's a she, sir.

"Yeah, okay, send *her* in."

"Sorry to barge in on you Mr. Tilden, I just have a few questions for you, sir. I won't keep you for very long, and I appreciate your seeing me."

"Always glad to help our police department, Detective Harris."

"Well, technically I work for the city of Chelan, sir."

"Did I forget to pay a parking ticket?"

"No sir. This is about a missing person report that was recently turned in to our department. You spoke to Father Damon O'Reilly about a man by the name of Brian Douglas. Is that correct?"

"Yes, I did. Is that a problem?"

"No sir. Quite frankly, it is you that we have to thank for initiating the hunt for him. Up to that time, no one realized the man was missing."

"Really? Then it was all by accident, I assure you. No one knew he was missing? Well just how long has Mr. Douglas been missing?"

"A while. My purpose in coming today to see you is why you wanted to talk to Brian Douglas?"

"Well, I build commercial buildings as well as residential homes. One of the homes I own was in need of some interior work and his reputation as a quality journeyman carpenter preceded him. I wanted to hire Mr. Douglas for that job."

"I see, he wasn't someone you had used before and knew," she asked.

"No, I didn't know him personally."

How did you happen to know that the Catholic priest knew him?"

"Detective Harris are you somehow implying that I might know the whereabouts of this Douglas man?"

"No sir, as I said before, I thank you for waking us up to his disappearance. I apologize if I insinuated that you might know something. I just have a couple of more questions and I'll get out your hair, sir. Do you know a man by the name of Tom Workman?"

"I know a lot of people. I'm not sure if I knew him. The name sounds familiar but I can't put a face to it. Should I know him?"

Detective Harris caught the past tense inference. "Well, not really. But by coincidence this man has been missing about the same amount of time as Mr. Douglas." I stood. "Well, I'd like to thank you Mr. Tilden for sharing your time with me and again I apologize for the interruption."

"The economy hasn't been good to the building trade Detective Harris and hope I haven't overreacted. You're welcome to ask me questions any time."

"You read my mind Mr. Tilden. I may be back in the future. Good day sir."

I walked out of the office and had reached the door when Mr. Tilden called after me.

"Please come back in Detective Harris," George Tilden said as he held the door open for me. "I remember where I know Tom Workman from. I play a little softball and Tom sometimes plays on our team. We don't play very much after it snows so that's the reason I couldn't connect the name. He's a mailman as I recall."

"That's right. His mother is the person who reported him missing. So you do know Tom Workman."

"Well, in the sense that I know who he is. I really don't know much about him. I know who he is and that he *was* a mailman."

"Do you recall the last time you saw him, sir?"

George shook his head. "I have trouble remembering what I had for breakfast this morning, but I'll work on that if it's important."

"It could be, so if you remember, here's my card. Thank you again."

I sat in my car recalling our conversation. The lieutenant was right. Tilden was smooth, but I had made him nervous and he screwed up a couple of times. I learned a long time ago that anyone can get nervous talking to a police officer. *So Mr. Workman was a softball player,* I thought. I knew where I would be going next on my hunt."

Tilden told his receptionist that he would be going out for lunch and might be gone for a couple of hours. The minute he entered his car, he called Bart Colangelo. They met at the Elks Club.

"I want you to call Vandy and find out what he's been saying about Tom, understand?" George demanded.

"What are you drinking George?" Bart called from the bar.

"Scotch and soda."

Bart ordered the drinks and set them o their table.

"I just had a detective in my office for about a half hour and something is going on. Call Vandy, and---.

"Settle down George," he interrupted, "you're starting to sound like a scared school girl. Tell me what the detective said."

George took a big hit of his drink. "Well, now that I think about it, maybe it was no big thing."

"Tell me what this detective asked you or what you talked about."

"Remember when I told you I had talked to the priest that knew Douglas."

"Yeah. What about it?"

"Well," and then he started laughing. In between fits of laughter he noticed that he had gotten the attention of two men at the bar. In a more hushed voice, "I panicked, sure as shit I panicked."

"Hopefully you didn't do it there, George."

"Come on Bart," he responded, a frown crossing his face. "Get me another scotch will you Bart."

"So maybe we'd better have a meeting with Vandy and try to come up with some answers for questions that may come our way."

"She doesn't know anything yet. Listen to this. I don't even think anyone knows that Brian Douglas has come into a lot of money.

"What makes you say that?"

"The priest didn't mention that Douglas had somehow acquired millions of dollars, and the detective didn't utter a word about money."

"Maybe that was done on purpose. Why should they tell you about it?"

"I don't know, but I don't think they know about his finances." George's cell phone started ringing. "Is that your phone Bart?"

"It's yours George."

"It's Vandy. Hello. A pause. "Who? He's already here; the Elks Club. George hung up. Guess who Vandy just talked to?"

"Who?"

CHAPTER TWELVE

"I'm glad you stopped by to see me Mr. Douglas. Things are looking up for you. Considering the terrible accident and aside from having most of your body busted up, I'd say you're a miracle man, as Dr. Son labeled you. Your recovery is spectacular and I'm not sugar coating it by any means. I believe that in the next couple of months you'll be ninety-nine percent of the man you once were, and that is saying a lot, sir. You've been an excellent patient and I wish you the very best. I'd like to personally thank you for the generous donation to the Alzheimer Charity in my name."

"You're welcome, sir. I don't know if I ever asked you why I have memory loss."

"Extra Axial spaces. These are lesions within the skull, but outside of the brain. Damage from Traumatic Brain Injury or TBI, can be focal, diffuse, or confined to specific areas. In your situation it is the damaged frontal lobe that can cause memory loss. We've given you CT scans and MRI's to determine whether it's a lesion, a chronic hematoma or something else. In your case we assessed it was hematoma, caused by your fall. We have been treating it with medication and I strongly believe that soon you won't be in need of the drug.

"So the pills that you gave me are to dissolve the blood clot in my head?"

Dr. Wolfe nodded, "that's about it. Yes. If you experience any dizziness at all; you have my card. Please call me anytime." We both stood. "I wouldn't consider learning to box or riding any dirt bikes, or engaging in any activity that would pound on your head, Mr. Douglas."

I nodded, "that sounds like good advice."

I was feeling good about Dr. Wolfe and all that he had done for me. I looked down at the pills that were bringing back my memories. I still had some empty spots but was getting better every day. It was strange that I had remembered my bank in the Cascade Mountains and then forgotten it again while I was here in the city. Dr. Wolfe couldn't explain the lapse but thought it was due to the hematoma in my head. I checked my watch. I was fifteen minutes early to see Dr. Dale. I sat down in the lobby without checking in with the receptionist. The doctor came around the corner with a cup of Starbucks coffee.

"Hey, there's that bionic man. Mr. Douglas, come on in. Would you like some coffee?"

"No thank you sir."

"Did you ever drink coffee?"

"Yes sir, I did. I think I have Dr. Son's uncle to thank for that change. I'm pretty much into drinking water, or fruit juice. I try to stay away from carbonated drinks."

"Dr. Son doesn't talk much about his uncle."

"Well, Tom Wah Gee is an incredible man, Dr. Dale. He's a real Shuai Chiao Monk. It's different kind of life, and it's not for everyone, but we could all learn from his life style."

"So you're about ready to go back to your home town…Chelan?"

"Yes sir."

"Is it possible you might have been in the military?"

"Dr. Dale, anything is possible. Dr. Lansing, my psychiatrist, has told to me, that some of my memory loss might be self induced. She believes I will regain my memory when I choose to remember my past."

"Well, I hope she's right. I've been through your town. It's small town living by a big lake, if I remember."

"It is. Lake Chelan."

Dr. Dale nodded. "You have a lot metal in you Mr. Douglas, so be aware you might have to step out of line at airports."

"Yes sir, I will. That you for everything you've done for me."

My next stop was going to be with Dr. Della Castani, my plastic surgeon, and I was just about on time.

"I'm here to see Dr. Castani."

"All right, Mr. Douglas, have a seat and she'll be with you in a few minutes."

"Wow, I can't believe the job I did on you Mr. Douglas," Dr. Castani raved as she observed his face as he sat down. "You might be the best surgery I've ever done."

"Aw shucks, Dr. Castani, you probably say that to all your patients," I joked.

"It's too bad I didn't have a picture of you. But in all honesty I have made you a real stud, Michael Douglas has nothing on you. Do you think anyone will recognize you back in your town?"

"I think I'm going to like my anonymity. It might play well for me for what I'd like to do.

"Well, if you find out you don't have a wife, please call me," she teased coyly.

"You love to embarrass me, don't you Dr. Castani? I am really pleased with your surgery. I think it has something to do with who I am now and I thank you. I'm sure you do very well for yourself. A beautiful, successful and very talented surgeon could sweep any man off his feet easily."

"Why thank you Mr. Douglas. Why doesn't my magic work on you?"

"It does. But, I'm a simple man with simple aspirations and you my dear, are more than I could ever handle."

"I think you're short changing yourself." She pulled him to her and kissed him hard for a few seconds. "You know where to find me, Brian Douglas," as she opened the door.

I found it hard to leave her office at that very moment, but I was running late and I hurried to my last appointment with Dr. Angie Lansing.

"I'm so glad you came to see me, Mr. Douglas. I was wondering if you had already left."

"'I wouldn't have left without seeing you Dr. Lansing. Did your daughter pick a college yet?"

"Not yet, but she has plenty of time to make that decision." She handed him a paper tissue. "I think your lip is bleeding," she chided. "You must have been to Dr. Costani's office."

"She is a naughty lady, but a wonderful surgeon. She does have a way about her though."

"Well, she is beautiful and completely without shame."

"Here, here."

"So I'm your last stop?"

I nodded.

"How's your memory doing?"

"I'm feeling pretty good about it. Dr. Wolfe gave me a new prescription to dissolve the blood clot in my head. He said I'm about ninety-nine percent there; should be all right in a couple of months. There are still some cobwebs in there, but they'll dissipate in time. Dr. Dale thought I might have been in some military organization because I call everybody sir. For the life of me I can't remember if I had some kind of military experience. I know where I lived now. Tomorrow I'll be there. It sounds exciting to think that after a little over a year I will be going home."

"Dr. Costani gave you a new face. Don't you wonder if you have any resemblance to your old one? How will any of your old friends know you? Does that worry you at all? Are you comfortable with dealing with all that you don't know?"

"I kind of went over all of those questions when Costani told me I would be getting a new face. I haven't been completely honest with you about me, Dr. Lansing. I will only say that I'm glad no one will recognize me. If someone that I don't want to know who I am ever finds out that I'm Brian Douglas, it might be fatal to all of the wonderful doctors here at the hospital. So even though I'm going home I may never be Brian Douglas again."

"My goodness Mr. Douglas, surely you're joking."

I smiled at Dr. Lansing, thinking it might be better not to appear serious. "Of course, I could never be anyone but Brian Douglas. Whoever said you can never go home again, was all wet. I'm going home again and I'm glad about it." I surprised Dr. Lansing when I approached, hugged, and kissed her on the cheek. She just looked at me in astonishment. "Thank you for all that you've done for me. If I ever need help again, I know I can count on you. I won't say goodbye," as I walked out her office smiling.

CHAPTER THIRTEEN

I never got tired of looking down at the Columbia River and finding the two bridges, the house on the corner of Cashmere and Ferry Streets, where I grew up, and of course the many orchards that looked like small patches of green lawn from the sky. Like all the towns and cities throughout the country, it was growing and constantly stretching its limits. The plane's tires bumping hard against the runway told me we had landed. As I deplaned I could feel the chill of fall against my face. I always looked for some familiar face as I scanned those waiting for the new arrivals of this flight. But as I walked through the electric doors I knew no one, and as I remembered Dr. Castani's words, "no one will know you darling, because I've made you someone else. You'll be invisible until you tell them who you are and despite yourself, you'll invite doubt." I walked into the men's bathroom, placed my duffle bag on the floor and looked up to see the face that was now mine staring back at me. The door opened, I looked away and walked to the urinal.

In my rental, I turned the radio on and then quickly turned it off. I didn't want any distraction. I wanted to take in all the changes that a year had brought to Wenatchee. Driving over the Obidasian Bridge I wondered if another lane had been added.

Heading north on Wenatchee Avenue, it seemed as though everything looked the same. I turned into the Best Western parking lot and I rented a room for a week. I was hoping I would see someone I knew, to try out my new face and identity.

I turned in early and the next morning jogged down to the Walmart turnoff and back, showered, ate a bowel of oatmeal and two slices of toast then was on my way to Chelan. The sun peaked over Badger Mountain while I drove the speed limit.

It was so peaceful, and even with some light traffic, my mind went back to my friend, Tom Wah Gee. I could envision him out in front of his cabin doing his stretches in a light robe. The gentle monk never knew cold. He never had to worry about traffic or meeting deadlines. The man had no worries. There was nothing for him to worry about.

The roadside sign indicated I would be entering Entiat in one mile. My mind came back to the present and my speed lowered to forty-five miles per hour. The Columbia runs south along the highway to Chelan and I was driving north. The drive through the tunnel created a surge of excitement in me because in just a few more minutes I would see Lake Chelan, which meant I would soon be home. As I reached the crest of the hill that guides you into the small town, I could see a small slice of the deep blue water of the fifty-mile long lake. I looked down at the speedometer. I was driving at eighty miles an hour. The road around the lake descended toward the level of the water. The hills surrounding the lake were now covered with grape vines. Chelanites were making their own wine.

Why not, if Californians can become famous for their winemaking grapes, then Washington with all its open land can follow suit. Though, I'm quite sure some of these wine makers were nothing more than transplanted Californians.

I was feeling euphoric with my arrival. The arms of the little lake town embraced me as I crossed the bridge and entered the main street. I glanced at the Senor Frog's building and wondered if Richard Montez, the owner of the beer establishment, would recognize the new me. Dr. Castani had once asked me if I thought my voice had changed. I was unable to answer the question for sure. It was still early and though the sun was out, it was chilly.

That's right, I thought, the throat doctor had examined me because of my raspy voice; he found a small lesion in my throat that looked like it had been there for a while. It was never determined conclusively that my voice had been altered because of the lesion. Was the tiny nodule there before my accident or had it appeared because of the accident? I guess it could matter, I thought. I walked only a short way before I felt the sting of early winter and hurried back to my car.

As I turned left on my old street, I drove slowly, allowing myself to think of the people that lived around me. On the right corner were the Medici's and next to them were the--- can't remember, or did I ever know. I couldn't think. A car behind me blew its horn for impeding traffic. I pulled over and looked down the street. Yes, yes, I remember Mrs. Latham, practically across the street. What was her first name? Latham…Latham, Virginia…no it was Heidi. Yeah! I remember. Yes! Heidi. I shouted. A woman walking by with a German Shephard on a leash stared at me from the sidewalk. I waved at her, she turned indignantly and sauntered off. My neurologist had said I would be closer to one hundred percent in about two months. Though she had stipulated that she was still a novice god and couldn't guarantee perfection. No matter, I remembered Hiedi Latham's name and could hardly wait to talk to her. I caught her looking over in my direction of few times. The more I thought about having talked to her, the more I doubted ever having had a conversation with her. That was all right, I had remembered her name. That was good. I drove by my house slowly, stopped in the middle of the sparsely traveled lanes, and stared at the poor, dejected, frail, lonely little bungalow. The small section of lawn was brown and neglected, as was the whole dwelling. I looked across at Mrs. Latham's house and saw her holding the curtain to one side, watching me. I stepped on the gas and drove forward.

Without thinking I found myself driving along the lake toward Manson, a small town at the opposite end of Chelan, and roughly fifty miles away. I wasn't going anywhere I wanted to go, so I turned around and drove until I stopped in front St. Anthony's church in Chelan. I was pretty sure I knew the priest in some way but his name wouldn't come to me. Suddenly there was a rapping on my side window. I looked up to see a priest standing there with a smile on his face. I rolled my window down.

"Are you Catholic, sir?" he asked.

I hesitated just a second. "Yes sir, I believe I am."

He smiled politely at me. "Well, that's a new one on me."

I opened my door and stepped out.

"Whoa, I meant no offense," the priest said backing away with his hands up. "None taken Father. I've been in this car for the last two hours, and I just need to stand for a few minutes."

"I don't recall seeing you around here before. I'm Father O'Reilly," as he extended his hand to me.

"Nice to meet you, Father."

"Ah, I didn't get your name."

"Oh, yeah, ah my, name is…Stewart Woods."

Father looked directly into my eyes. "Are you sure about that, Mr. Woods?" He was still staring at me when, practically in unison, we burst out laughing.

"Sorry about that, Father. I recently spent some time in a hospital after a very bad accident and it takes me a few seconds to recall things."

"Sorry to hear that. I assume you live in Chelan."

"No sir, I don't, but I'm thinking about moving here. I flew in on Horizon yesterday and I'm staying in Wenatchee until I can find somewhere suitable to live."

"I don't know how much you know about the housing market here in Chelan, Mr. Woods, but it has gotten expensive in the last few years."

"I am aware of the prices. I spent some time here a few years ago and like your small town."

"I'll be right back Mr. Woods," he called out as he hurried off to the church.

I turned to the hillside and lost myself in thought. It's strange about one's memory, but mine was scoping in on my friendship with Father O'Reilly. I remember our trips to see the Seahawks play and that he was a baseball fan. That he was a God fearing man, but never seemed like a priest. Even on Sundays when I would see him in the pulpit, he didn't present the image of a priest. The parishioners loved the gentle man.

"Have I lost you Mr. Woods?" he asked as he approached quietly from behind me.

"No sir, I was just thinking that I should be getting back to Wenatchee. I have something I must do."

"Here's a schedule of our masses. By the way, St. Joseph's Catholic church is no longer on Chelan Street in Wenatchee."

"Yes Father. I know where it is, can't remember the name of the street, but I know I could find it."

"Good. Well I hope you find a good home here."

"Me too, Father." I started to drive away when he asked me, "Are you a sports fan, Mr. Woods?"

"I sure am, Father. See ya."

The drive back to Wenatchee was faster than the drive up to Chelan. It's strange how that always seems to be.

I was hungry and made the decision to have some red meat. I drove into the Windmill parking lot on Wenatchee Avenue. It hadn't changed in years. It still had the big fans, like a windmill, part of its lure.

"Yes sir, are you expecting any others tonight?"

"No, it's just me. I understand you have the best steaks in town."

"Completely true sir. One look at this body and you'll know it's true," she said and stood to one side for me to check out.

She had a marvelous figure."

"Do you eat the potato too?" I asked with a smile.

"No, just the steak and the salad, no dressing."

"Sounds great. Would you do me the honors of ordering the steak you like with the potato, and salad with Italian dressing."

"Coming right up, sir. Did you want a glass of wine with your dinner?"

"A good red house wine will be fine."

The waiter sat me in the back where the lighting was dim. There were two couples in the area where I was seated. My thoughts went back to Father O'Reilly. He had no idea who I was. I had pulled it off. I feel like a stinking coward for deceiving him, but it might save his life in the long run. I wanted to maintain anonymity and remain dead. What I was going to be doing from now on was finding those responsible for my trip to the Cascade Mountains. I sipped my wine and saw the restaurant was getting busy. I could hear different voices talking quietly when suddenly I heard someone say "Tilden". I looked to see if I could discern who had uttered the name. I stood and walked in the direction of the bathrooms, looking toward the front table where I suspected the name had been voiced. I reached the bathroom, washed my hands and returned to my table. *Maybe it just sounded like "Tilden,"* I thought.

CHAPTER FOURTEEN

I was shivering uncontrollably and it was either early morning or evening. I was almost certain what I was staring at were not big dogs. They were about ten feet apart, looking in my direction. I could only see three. The tree I was leaning against was partially dead and had few pine needles on the limbs. I sensed that I was what they were after, but so far, no one was doing anything about it. I looked down and around, searching for rocks or large broken limb. It seemed crazy to me that they would want me, but there was no one else around. I didn't realize how scared I was until I felt something warm running down my legs. I looked down and saw urine racing over my boot and coloring the snow yellow. Then I saw a three-inch in diameter dead branch, started toward it and fell. The three wolves all started moving slowly in my direction. I grabbed the large piece of wood and stood quickly. Then, oh my God, these weren't dogs: these were hungry---Wolves! Now that I knew what they were I felt panic. How did I get out here? Of course I knew why they were staring at me. I was going to be their next meal. My God, I can't believe I did this. Why? How far had I wondered from the cabin? Was Gee looking for me? How long had I been gone? The shaking had gotten so bad I could hardly hold the limb in my hand and was getting dizzy. I edged back to the tree and leaned against it again. The wolves moved closer and as the limb fell from my hand the three wolves sprang.

"Ahhhh," I screamed and sat up in my bed. I was shaking and the sweat was pouring out. There was a loud knocking on my door.

"Hey! You all right in there?"

I opened the door in my boxer shorts and stared at a young man and woman.

"Yes, I'm sorry. I guess I had a bad dream. Thank you for your concern, I'm all right now."

"You sure?" the woman asked. "Are you alone in there?"

"Yes. I'm fine," and I closed the door. It would be like Tom Wah Gee, not to mention to his nephew that I had been close to becoming those wolves lunch. It wasn't the first time I had dreamed the same scene. Did I only dream I had been attacked by hungry wolves?

I took out my note pad and wrote myself a note about the wolves.

I wanted to go back to Chelan and talk to Mrs. Latham and some of the other neighbors, but I also wanted to take in some of Wenatchee. Just drive around the streets and maybe have lunch at some restaurant where I had never eaten. The old part of town itself is small, about three or four blocks square. Most of the newer shopping centers were away from the old town. After I had driven around the residential streets and to the old high school, which was now residential housing. I decided to drive to Chelan.

I drove up to Mrs. Latham's and parked on the street in front of her house. It was only then that I wondered if she would be home.

The door opened before I had the chance to knock.

"Yes sir, what can I do for you?"

"Does anyone live in the house across the street?"

"Well, I'll tell you. Come in. Do you have a few minutes to talk? My name is Heidi Latham." She walked him into her kitchen and poured two cups of coffee. "How do you drink it?"

"Like it is."

She sat across the small table from me.

"You the one that stopped to look at Brian's house yesterday?"

I nodded, "It looked like it wasn't occupied."

"Well, here's the thing. Not one word has been said about that house or Brian Douglas, Mr.…"

"Woods, Stewart"

"Mr. Woods, now everyone's looking for information about Brian, the man that lives in that house. Pretty strange, huh? I'm guessing it's about a year since the man vanished; right into thin air. No one heard from him since. Now the police are looking for him. The local catholic priest and a schoolteacher friend are talking to all the neighbors."

"When did you find out he was missing?"

"I'm one of the few that knew he worked for the government. I just figured he might have gone back to work for them and that's why he wasn't around. It wasn't till the priest came around asking about him and that's only been about two or three weeks now."

I have to admit I wasn't very sociable. No reason for it, just the way I was, I thought.

"Brian was a very bright man. Had a good college education and did good for his mother and father when they were alive."

I nodded. "Is that a guitar over in the corner, Mrs. Latham?"

"Please call me Heidi, it's friendlier. Yes, my husband played it. He's been gone for a while now. It just sits where he used to leave it. You play?"

"Yes, but I haven't played for some time now."

"I think that Father O'Reilly and Brian became good friends because they both played a good guitar. Yes sir, they both have good voices and can sing as well as they played."

"Do you have any idea what might have happened to Mr. Douglas?"

"None. I just hope he's still alive. He's in my prayers, Mr. Woods."

"Do you know if he had any financial problems?"

"I really don't think so. He made a lot of money working for the government."

I really was able to keep a low profile, I thought.

"Did you say you knew him, Mr. Woods?"

"No, I didn't know this Brian Douglas, Heidi. My initial interest was in his home. I thought if the house was available, I would look into possibly purchasing it."

"Well, I haven't heard anything about it being for sale on account no one has said he's passed on. Just no one knows where Brian Douglas is. But don't take my word for whether his house is for sale. For all I know and that isn't much, it could be. The people across the street and down at the corner might know.

They're the Medici's, Roger and Lilly and Katie Lawson lives three doors down from me, might know something. She used to work for a real estate company. Will Duggan and his wife, Mary Beth knew the mailman pretty well. You might get some information from them."

I gave Heidi a puzzled look.

"Did I confuse you about something Mr. Woods?"

"Well…you lost me with the mailman."

She nodded. "That's right. It was Father O'Reilly and Christina Palmer, I told about the mailman. I knew who he was, but the Duggan's knew him and his mother better. I don't recall her first name though," and Heidi stopped talking.

"Was there something I should know about the mailman?"

"Oh my gosh, I guess I had a senior moment there Mr. Woods. I was leading you there to tell you that Father Damon. Christina and I believe he disappeared in the same week, if not the same day."

"Are you saying that the mailman and this Brian Douglas might have vanished at the same time?"

"Well, I'm not sure that I'm saying that. I think what I'm saying is the same thing might have happened to both of them."

I smiled. "Well, do think the mailman is still alive?"

"Mr. Woods, his mother reported him missing two or three days later because he *was* our letter carrier. He had a job. Brian had a job too, but it was more of a hobby than something he needed to pay his monthly bills. I don't know if Tom's alive or not but it's more spooky about him. The post office had to get someone new to deliver the mail. His mother thinks someone killed him." She stood and walked out of the kitchen and was gone for few minutes.

"Here's Loretta Workman's address and the addresses of the neighbors I mentioned earlier. I'm not sure about the Medici's address, but they're the ones that live in the corner house across the street. The white house with the brown trim and Blue Spruce in the front yard, you can't miss it."

Her body language was telling me she was through talking to me and she walked me to the door.

"It has been interesting talking to you Mrs. Latham. I owe you a cup of coffee and will be glad to take to Starbucks at our next meeting."

"I did notice you didn't drink the cup I poured you."

"You're right. I don't drink coffee very often, but that doesn't mean I didn't appreciate the cup I didn't drink."

Puzzled. "I guess I understand what you've just said, Mr. Woods."

Smiling at her, "We'll meet again Mrs. Latham." Walking to my rental car I viewed my house again and got that lump in my throat. It looked so lonely and forlorn and unkempt. I drove away wishing I hadn't looked across the street.

It was almost time to eat. My stomach was starting to grumble. Loretta Workman's house looked quiet. I rang the doorbell and stood looking away from the door. At least a minute passed and I was about to leave when it opened.

"Mrs. Workman?"

"Yes, I'm Mrs. Workman. Who are you?"

"Ah, Mrs. Latham sent me."

"Oh Heidi sent you? Yes, come in. Are you with the police?"

"No I'm not."

"You know my son's been missing for a year now and, and no one knows a damn thing. The PD says it's because of the economy. I don't know what this world's coming to," she walked to the kitchen counter, grabbed a tissue and blew her nose. "Can you believe it? A whole year, he's been missing and still not one word. The strange thing is that another man on his mail route is missing. We figured that the two of them disappeared about the same day. A whole year, oh my God, and no one has any answers." She began weeping and walked away. I could hear her blowing her nose. She came back a few minutes later carrying a picture.

"This is Tom," as she handed me the picture.

I froze. I was looking at the man that had fallen out of the plane. I dropped the picture and hurried to the door, opened it and rushed out. I was sitting in my car when Mrs. Workman tapped on my window. I looked up and lowered the glass. "I'm sorry Mrs. Workman. I'm afraid I can't explain my actions. I'm sorry." We walked back into her house. "About all I can say in my defense, is that I recently spent some time in the hospital for an accident I had." I sat down where she had seated me before.

"Would you bring your son's picture back again? I would like to look at it."

I looked at the face and knew where I had seen it. All this time I had not known. Now I remembered the plane and what subsequently happened to me. I knew what had happened to Tom Workman. Dr. Lansing had said that this would happen. That I would remember and then try to forget it again because…

"Here sir." She handed me a glass of liquid.

"What is it?"

"Whiskey." I looked at it and took a sip.

"Drink it all," she commanded.

I poured it down. I hadn't eaten anything I could feel the liquid numbing my body. I was relaxing. Tom workman had fallen out of the plane by accident, but my exit had been on purpose. "Mrs. Workman, I have to go. Thank you for the drink. I needed that. I promise to talk to you again. I don't know when, but we will be seeing each other again." I stood and walked carefully to the door.

"Are you going to be all right driving?" she asked, opening it for me.

"Thank you, I'll be all right."

Mrs. Workman returned her son's picture to the bedroom and sat at the kitchen table, then, suddenly she stood quickly and rushed to the door. She stood looking where the man had parked. He was gone. *I don't think I ever asked him his name,* she thought.

CHAPTER FIFTEEN

Twenty eight days later, George Tilden and Bart Colangelo were waiting for Vandy Earhart to show up at the Elks Club.

"It's probably nothing George. This guy jumps at his own shadow."

"I don't know Bart, this time he was really spooked."

"Meeting here was a good idea, it's dead right now," Bart mused looking around.

"Here he comes. He even looks all stressed out," George pointed out.

Vandy sat down and looked around. "We've got problems and---"

"Would you like a drink, Vandy?" Bart cut in.

"No, yes, yes, I'll have a double shot of JD on the rocks."

Bart set the Jack Daniel's drink on the table. "Now take a deep breath and tell us what you've heard."

Vandy told George and Bart about a man that had been to Loretta workman's house and talked about Tom. Mrs. Workman was pretty sure he knew Tom.

"What's the man's name?" Bart asked.

" Well, there's the rub. She didn't get his name."

"Come on Vandy. She didn't get his name,"

"She probably made the whole thing up to scare the shit out of you, Vandy," George chimed in.

"I don't know. I don't think she made it up," Vandy said defensively. The thing is, he's not the only one that has taken an interest in Tom Workman."

"What? Spit it out. Who else is sniffing around?"

Vandy felt intimidated by the two staring at him. "Well, there's a new detective snooping around, plus a priest and a woman."

"What do you mean a new detective?"

"I told you that a detective had talked to me about Tom Workman's disappearance, right after the whole thing happened. Right Bart?"

Bart nodded. "Yeah, what about this priest and the woman. Is the priest the guy you talked to George?"

"If it's Father Damon O'Reilly, then it's the same man."

Vandy nodded.

"Who's the woman?"

Vandy retrieved a small note pad. "Her name is Christina Palmer. She teaches at Chelan High School. What I heard from one of Brian's neighbor's is that she hired Brian to do some carpentry work."

George leaned forward in his chair. "I don't get it. Are you telling me that Douglas was working as a carpenter for peanuts when he was loaded with millions of dollars?"

"One more thing, George. I don't think anyone knew he had all this money," Vandy volunteered.

"Did you know this Bart?"

"No I didn't, but now that I think about it. We haven't heard a single word about any money. Somebody besides us knew he had money and yet no one has come forward. Nothing in the paper or any where else; pretty strange."

They stopped talking and sat ruminating what was just said. Bart stood and walked to the bar. "Three more of the same."

Vandy spoke first. "Mrs. Workman is pretty sure Tom is dead."

George took a big drink of JD, "Why would she think that, Vandy?"

"Come on George. It's been a year since---"

"So what?" George interrupted.

"Have you eaten anything today, George?" Bart asked.

"I had breakfast."

"Let's go have a steak somewhere," Bart suggested.

"Yeah," George muttered.

"You guys go ahead. I've got something else to do," Vandy gulped his drink and hurried out ahead of George and Bart.

"What do you think, Bart?"

"Vandy's all right."

"You believe all that shit he said."
"Yeah, I'm afraid I do."

CHAPTER SIXTEEN

I rented a home on Badger Mountain Road in East Wenatchee and paid for three months. I don't mind motels but homes are more private and I was still a private person. I wanted to call Dr. Lansing about my memory break-through and the pill I was taking.

Mrs. Latham had been most informative, but she knew my name and I was sure she would mention it to the police detective and anyone else that was looking for Tom Workman or Brian Douglas.

I still had the short manuscript that Dr. Son Lo Gee had written to me when I was in the Cascade Mountains. It was starting to show wear from opening and closing. This written testimony had been my motivation for finding out what happened to me. I was now aware of the plane ride, without detail however, that Tom Workman's picture had evoked on my memory. Does memory work with a small piece of a picture that comes into view as memory unfolds, more faces, and why I was even on the plane? Is that what it does? Somehow, as I thought of Dr. Lansing, I knew the answer would surely become more complex.

I pondered Dr, Gee's words again, "I don't know if you will eventually succumb to all your injuries and they are many, or survive long enough for me to one day see and talk to you again. I only hope that my uncle rescued a good man and not a felon on the run."

Was I a felon on the run? Where did I get all the money I have, I wondered. How did I remember I had an account in a Seattle bank, but couldn't remember Tom Workman until very recently or the plane ride. I paid all the doctor bills and no one had come after me, so the funds must be legit. Had I stolen the money, or maybe inherited it? I decided to take a run and get my mind on a different plane. The run cleared my mind.

There was something else I wanted to do. I had recently turned fifty and wanted to get back in shape. I had once been in very good shape and wanted to feel that way again.

After a week of trying to find a good professional trainer, I hired a woman that was five years older than me. However, she looked at least ten years younger. What sold me on Rachel Susanne Harvey was that she had once boxed Mohammed Ali's daughter, and lost of course. But now I had a trainer that would get me back to the shape I was in at twenty-five years of age again, well, maybe thirty-five.

Twelve days later I woke up and gulped down two Advil. Every muscle in my body hurt. It even hurt to walk. The down side of soreness was that the drill instructor that I hired would soon be here for another session.

I had parked my car at State Park, near the lake, gone swimming and then changed my clothes in the facility nearest my car.

As I seated myself and inserted the keys in the ignition, I noticed a note under my windshield wipers. Looking around, I stepped out and picked the note up. Again I scanned the area for someone that might be watching me. I saw a man peek around one of the evergreen trees that are abundant in the park. He appeared to be looking directly at me. I opened the note. It read, 'I would like to talk to you Mr. Woods.' He walked out from behind the tree that hid him and walked toward me. "You are Stewart Woods aren't you?"

I nodded, confused.

"We have a mutual friend and that's how I know your name," he said.

I could only think of two people I had told my name.

"I have Tourette's Syndrone, but I'm not crazy. My ticks are mostly neck twists and grunting, but that's about all. Some people take those things to mean you're crazy. I'm not crazy. I've tied my bike to that tree over there and wondered if we could take a ride in your car while we talk."

"What are we going to talk about?" I asked.

"Tom Workman and Brian Douglas, I think I know what happened to them."

"Hop in," I said excitedly.

"What's your connection to Brian Douglas, Mr. Woods?" he inquired.

"Should I have some connection to him?"

"Let's not be coy Mr. Woods."

"I don't know your name. How do you know mine?"

"Mrs. Latham told me your name."

I nodded, "All right, I did talk to her."

"Look, I'm on your side. There's enough mystery to go around. Let's cut to the quick. I think Tom is dead and very possibly Mr. Douglas. For a while I thought you might be Brian Douglas until I saw a picture of Brian. Tom told me some stuff a couple of weeks before he disappeared that were very interesting. I wanted to make sure you were not on the side of George Tilden. I think he's part of this whole thing. At least, Tom Workman said some things that tie George Tilden to Tom Workman. I firmly believe he had something to do with this whole business, but I don't have any proof. I'm trusting that you don't have any affiliation with Tilden, cause if you do, I'm a walking dead man."

"I'm the least of your worries, but why are you sticking your neck out for Tom Workman?"

"He was a very good friend. I'm a few years older than Tom, but never the less we were the best of friends." He grunted several times and jerked his head. I know it's hard to talk to someone with no name, so you can call me Cal. Okay?"

"Well Cal, you took a big chance talking to me. I am definitely on your side. After this meeting I don't think we should meet again unless it's paramount to finding out who abducted Workman and Douglas. If the wrong people find out we've talked, both of our lives could be in jeopardy."

"Who are you really, Mr. Woods?"

"I don't think I should tell you, Cal. Not knowing who I am might save your life one day."

"All right, the thing is Mr. Woods, I'm not a brave man. I've watched to many CSI's, and Law and Order. I don't want to show my hand and die for it. I'm not smart enough to snoop around and stay alive. I just haven't had anybody to talk to about it and I was hoping you were that man. I thought that if you were Brian Douglas, we could collaborate, I think that's the right word. If you weren't, I was thinking you might be FBI or CIA; one of those government agents with some clout. You know what I mean?"

"Well, Cal I'm none of those things. I'm pretty much in the same boat you're in. I'm trying to keep a low profile for the same reasons. Though I'm really glad to have you as an ally. I think we can help each other. You were right about having our conversation in this car. I think we should keep the same vigilance from now on. Every meeting should be treated like our lives depend on it, because I believe it does."

"I'm pretty sure there's something you're not telling me Mr. Woods, but I trust you will tell me at some time in the future."

Cal extended his hand over to me and we shook them, in sealing the alliance.

Driving back to Wenatchee, I thought about our conversation. I wanted to know where Cal had obtained a picture of Brian Douglas. I know there was a picture of me in the paper when I went to work for ATF, but that was years ago. The only other pictures were in the Chelan High School yearbook, but that was even longer. No matter, I liked Cal and I believe he was sincere about all that he said, including the real fear he felt from all that was happening and could happen. The name Tilden kept popping up and somehow I felt like I should know something about the person. I made the decision to go to Mass in Chelan this Sunday. I wanted to talk to Father O'Reilly. I had a schedule of the masses and the priest that would say them.

I sat in a rear pew through the mass and then walked a short way from the church to allow the priest to greet his congregation. After the last parishioner had shaken his hand, I approached him.

"I didn't see you in the communion line this morning, Mr. Woods."

"It's been a while since I've been to the confessional box, Father. I'll make it a point to go this coming Saturday. I was wondering if I could take you someplace for lunch or breakfast?

"Sounds great. Would you mind going to Denny's Restaurant, they have the best pancakes and Belgium Waffles."

I nodded.

"I'll change and be out in few."

Fifteen minutes later they were seated at Denny's Restaurant , and had ordered Belgium waffles, coffee, and juice.

"So what's on your mind, Mr. Woods? Did you find a place to live?"

"I did Father, I think I mentioned that I had been in a hospital recently, and had some memory loss from an accident."

"Yes, you did tell me that."

Well, recently I had a flash of memory that has evoked something from the past. It's just a small piece of memory; it begs more questions.

"I have an idea. I'm going to call a friend of mine and ask her if we could come over for a home cooked breakfast, and we can talk freely. Would you object?"

"I don't know, Father..."

"She's one of us, I assure you it will be all right."

The next morning as they entered Christina's house, "Wow, you brought enough food for an Army, Father. Set the bags on the counter. Is it breakfast or lunch?" She called out to me, "I'm Christina Palmer."

"Woods, Stewart Woods. It's really nice of you to do this."

"Father did you say you wanted breakfast or lunch?," she asked.

"I'll have what ever you two choose."

"Stewart?"

"Ah, breakfast is fine with me."

"Breakfast it is."

We sat around the table, thoroughly stuffed. "Christina, I can't remember the last time I ate like this."

"Ditto," Father smiled.

"Let me understand this. The reason you two birds ended up here, was because you, Stewart wanted to find out something about memory loss."

"I already told Father about my stay in a hospital in Seattle. A recent visit to one of the neighbors here in Chelan, broke through my memory when I remembered that I had been on a plane, and that somehow Tom Workman was involved. Now I hear that he has disappeared from Chelan. The presumption is that he is dead."

"The neighbor told you this?" Father O'Reilly probed.

"Yes. She believes he's dead."

"How long have you had this memory loss, Stewart?" Christina asked.

"Over a year. I think I should tell you this before we go any further. You two are going to have to trust me. There are some things I can't talk to you about because...well, because, it might put you in danger."

Christina leaned forward in her chair. "Do you know that Father and I are working with a local detective. We're all trying to find out what happened to those two men. We didn't know Tom Workman at all, but Father and I were close to Brian Douglas. Father has known him since he was a kid and they were quite the musical duo, with wonderful voices to boot, I hear."

I was embarrassed. Here I was, knowing I was Brian Douglas but for the sake of me, I couldn't remember either one of them. I thought, *Dr. Lansing could probably explain this.*

Father O'Reilly spoke up. "You know Stewart, I think you can trust Christina and me because we've always had Brian Douglas's best interests at heart. We believe he's still alive. We think because we haven't heard about him...well, no news is good news."

It was tempting to tell them who I really was, but at the same time, it could be disastrous for all of us.

"What did Mr. Douglas do for a living? What kind of friends did he have? Have you talked to any of them? How long has the detective you mentioned been working on this. Does anyone know anything at all about what has happened to him? How did…did he know Tom Workman? What did Workman do for a living?" I couldn't stop asking questions and my voice kept getting louder. I put my hands to my face, stood and walked outside.

Father and Chris looked at each other, perplexed.

After a few seconds I came back. "I'm sorry for the outburst. The medication I take has some side affects."

CHAPTER SEVENTEEN

A week had passed since my outburst at Christina Palmer's home and I was waiting for a return call from my Neurologist, Dr. Michael Wolfe. The phone finally rang.

"Brian, Dr. Wolfe."

"Thanks for returning my call Dr. Wolfe." I explained how some of my memory had returned and then the outpouring at a social visit with some friends. " Do you think it's possible that the medication I'm taking is causing sudden inappropriate eruptions?"

"Have you had more than one of those outbursts?"

"No, but I have felt some tension at different times and managed to quell what might have turned into an episode."

"Brian, before I consider changing your medication, I would like to refer you to Dr. Lansing. She might be able to give you a more personal answer to your question. Mine is more perspective, and the meds I'm giving you are to dissipate any lesions in your head from your accident. If she isn't able to give you the answers you want to hear, have her call me and I'll consider changing your meds, all right? Do you have her number Brian?"

"I do. Thank you Dr. Wolfe."

Did I really need to call Lansing? Wolfe gave me the impression that it wasn't the pills. I was on the fence about calling Dr. Lansing, so I took a thirty-minute run and when I returned called her on her cell phone, which got me a 'not available at this time,' message. I left my cell number and waited.

I drove down Badger Mountain Road, across the bridge and found myself parking at one of the stops of 'the Loop.' The loop was a path that circled from the old bridge to the new bridge covering both sides of the Columbia River. It was asphalt paved and gave citizens from East Wenatchee and Wenatchee a few miles of room to exercise. There was always someone walking or running on the lane, even in the winter. I was wearing a pair of Adidas workout pants and Nike running shoes, but I didn't want to run. I had already done my hour today and I didn't want to sweat.

The chill in the air was perfect for a walk and I was off. My mind went back to the day I went swimming in Lake Chelan and my odd meeting with Cal. He had an affliction that I'm sure is treated with some type of medication. He had probably been living with it for years and it didn't seem to bother him. He had just shucked it off with, "I have Tourette's Syndrome but I'm not crazy." I smiled to myself when I remember him barking quietly one time while we were together. Again, he made nothing of it and just went on talking.

I was in need of assessing my self. Number one, I was reasonably sure I was Brian Douglas, at least at this very moment, I was. Two, Dr. Son Do Gee, had recommended and was affirmed, by Dr. Lansing, that I should have an alias before I went back to the place I had called home. I had opened an account in a bank in Seattle months before I ended up in Tom Wah Gee's cabin, out in the wilderness of the Cascade Mountains. The address I had placed on the account was in Chelan, Washington. Three, I still had no idea where the money came from other than the explanation by the banks president that it was a lottery check. Four, I remembered Tom Workman's face from Mrs. Workman's picture and the plane, but that was all. I was getting tired of the bits and pieces of my inconsistent memory.

I walked up to the new north-end bridge and back. I checked my cell phone and hopped into my car and started home. The phone began ringing. I drove to the side of the road and parked.

"Dr. Lansing, thanks for getting back to me. I put her on speakerphone?

"Is everything all right Brian? I just finished talking to Dr. Wolfe."

"I'm not sure. I don't want to sound like some whiney kid, but I guess I'm going to anyway. I've been having these anxiety attacks, nothing big, but it throws me off. I told Dr.

Wolfe I thought it might be the pills I'm taking. What do you think?"

"There is a remote possibility that it could be the meds, but I agree with Dr. Wolfe, it's more likely *all* that has happened to you is percolating and coming to the top now. You have been traumatized severely by the accident and all the surgeries that you have endured. Brian, your going to have some odd episodes. I suppose I could prescribe some Valium or some sort of sedative that would calm you, but your taking a lot of different pain pills, now."

"I think you're telling me to gut it out. I think I can handle it. It does make sense, I mean what you just said. Yeah, I have had a lot happen to me. OK, I'll gut it out."

"Have you made any progress?"

"Not really Dr. Lansing. I'm glad we're talking. Do you think I might be afraid to pursue what happened to me?"

"What do you think, Brian?"

"I don't know. Sometimes I feel like I'm not going after it like I should. Like maybe, I don't want to know. Yet, I want to know. Does that make sense?"

"It's not unusual for a person that has gone through what you have, to try to forget about it. Are you afraid?"

"No, I don't think I'm afraid of the unknown. I don't that for a fact, but it's how I feel."

"If it means anything to you Brian, I don't think you're afraid either."

"Thanks Dr. Lansing, it does, it means a lot to me. Hey, thanks for calling back. I'm glad I called."

"Sorry it took so long to get back to you Brian."

"It's okay, Bye."

"Brian, joining a health club would be good. Just no boxing."

"Yeah, okay, no boxing. Thanks again."

I sat for a few seconds and thought about Dr. Lansing words to me. I smiled and drove home with new enthusiasm. Maybe I was a little afraid. Somebody crapped on me and I don't like it. What is it that guy said in the movie? "I'm mad as hell, and I'm not going to take it anymore." I rolled my window down and yelled, "I'm mad as hell and I'm not going to take it anymore," and began laughing to myself.

Dr. Lansing was right. I had been through a lot. I'm still going through a lot. I know I'm not afraid. I could be willfully trying to forget my rotten ordeal. That made sense. Falling from a bike, or horse, or while learning to ski, isn't quite like falling from a plane and breaking most of the big bones in your body, as well as whole lot of the small ones, but the results are the same. You have to get up and try it again if you're going to succeed. Not that I wanted to fall out of plane again, I certainly was from that philosophy.

Half way up Badger Mountain Road, on my way home, I stopped, turned around and headed for Target. I picked up some note pads, a role of white paper, regular and colored pencils, and some pens. I was going to get serious about finding out what has happened to me. I rushed home and attached a large section of the marking paper to the wall of the extra bedroom.

I wanted to write down everything I knew about myself: as well as what I didn't know. I wanted to see it on paper where I could look at it and know for sure what I knew. Trying to keep information in my head was just too much. I was hoping I could develop a plan from my notes to go after the people that did this to me. Justice. First on my list was George Tilden. I had to find out who this man was and how he fit into this whole thing.

Father O'Reilly had mentioned the name once and so had Cal. I went to my Apple Computer and looked up Tilden Commercial and Residential Properties. I wrote down his business address and made some other notations on Mr. Tilden.

The doorbell rang, which surprised me. I looked out the peephole and saw an attractive woman looking directly at the peephole. I opened the door.

"Mr. Stewart Woods?"

"Yes,"

"I'm Detective Marci Harris, from the Chelan Police Department. Would it be possible to talk to you for a few minutes sir?"

"Come in Detective." I led her to the kitchen. "Would you like a cup of coffee or tea?"

"No thanks, I've had my two cups today," she responded easily, and pulled a note pad from her purse.

"Would you mind if we sat here at the kitchen table?" I requested.

"Not at all."

"How did you get my name, Detective Harris?"

"Father O'Reilly and Christina Palmer gave me that information."

I nodded.

"I understand you're from Seattle and that you spent some time in a hospital there."

I was getting anxious again. I remember telling Father O'Reilly that. Did she do some checking with the hospital?

"Yes, that's right."

"I'm just curious. What's your interest in Brian Douglas?"

I thought I had anticipated all the possible questions one might ask me. But what's my interest? I couldn't think of a thing. I threw up my hands. "I didn't realize I had shown real interest, just curiosity. I meet two good people and they become my friends. Then they pour out this story that got me curious. What can I say, Detective?"

She nodded. "I thought you were going to live in Chelan."

"That's true, I'm renting here until I can find a place in there."

"What kind of work do you do Mr. Woods?"

"I'm retired, and living off a small inheritance."

"Do you have a family in Seattle?"

"No ma'am, I don't. I think I'm the last of my clan."

She put her pen down on the table. "Woods, is that German?"

"No ma'am, we were Irish, but I know some Woods that are German."

"I could only guess at what nationality you are detective?"

"And what would you guess?"

"Nowadays, it is very difficult to determine a person's ethnicity, but if I had to speculate, I would say Italian, because of your dark hair and brown eyes."

"Close, but no cigar, Mr. Woods. I'm half Pamunkey Indian."

"Wow, then you must be a transplanted Pamunkey Indian."

"I am Mr. Woods." Her cell phone rang. She answered and then stood and put her note pad away. "I have to run. I hope I don't have to arrest you some day sir, because you seem like a nice man," as she hurried to the door.

"I hope so too, Detective Harris," I said from the doorway as she entered her car.

I walked back to the kitchen, then into the spare bedroom and to the wall, where I put the name 'Detective Marci Harris next to George Tilden.' I smiled to myself and thought I was finally making progress.

I was glad Detective Harris had come to check me out. If I was going to find out what happened to me, it was important law enforcement had my back. Snooping around wasn't going to be as much of a worry. I wasn't alone anymore. Maybe I should let Harris and my friends know who I really am. I thought about that for a few seconds. On the other hand, whoever did this to me, was playing hardball.

I drove down the hill to Tilden Enterprise. 2312 North Wenatchee Avenue was a prosperous looking building. George Tilden was obviously a successful businessman. His residence address was unlisted, so I fraudulently obtained it by pretending to be Federal Express. I drove up one of the canyon roads on the Wenatchee side and found a large ranch style home and a beautiful red barn. There was a corral behind the house where several horses were grazing on hay. *The man had a taste for the better things,* I thought.

As I turned the car around I saw a woman walking to the barn. I thought Mr. Tilden would be working, so I stopped and took out my note pad, scribbled an address on it, got out of my car, and started walking to the barn.

She turned around and saw me, and waited till I was close.

"Yes sir. What can I do for you?"

"I'm not sure. Would you know if this address is in this area?" I asked as I handed her the address.

"I think you're lost sir. I don't recognize the road. It might be the next canyon over, but I don't think so. Sorry I'm not able to help you," and she returned the address to me.

"Do you have the name of the people you are looking for?"

"Dalrimple," I lied.

She repeated the name, shook her head, "I don't recognize the name. Your welcome to use my phone if you have a number to call."

"I'm afraid I don't."

"Would you like to use the phone book?"

I could see she really wanted to help.

"I'm not sure they have a phone. These people are very private, however, it couldn't hurt to look."

"My name is Diane Tilden."

"Stewart Woods."

"Nice to meet you Stewart," extending her hand. I took it. "Thank you for being so gracious," she smiled at me, and I looked down at our hands still locked in a handshake.

"Oh, sorry," she apologized and released my hand. "The kitchen is straight ahead. I'll get the phone book."

"The only Dalrimple is in East Wenatchee and it's not them. Thank you for taking the time to help a stranger, Mrs. Tilden."

"Diane, please. You *must* let me know if you find them Stewart. We're not in the phone book so I'm giving you my card."

I looked at the card. "George and Diane Tilden?"

"Yes, and George is always working or on a business trip, or taking some one hunting or fishing. He has his own plane and can be gone on a minute's notice."

"I'll remember that, Diane. Thanks again," and I left her smiling at the front door.

As I drove out of the canyon, I thought Diane Tilden might be lonely. Her nearest neighbor had to be at least a hundred yards away. I also think she was flirting with me. Now, I had to talk to Father O'Reilly. Once I got to Wenatchee Avenue, I pulled to the side of the road and called.

I met the priest at a little restaurant off the main street; he ordered coffee, I took water. "Thanks for meeting with me Father. Like I told you and Miss Palmer, I'm retired and live on a modest inheritance. I'm in no hurry to find a place to live here in Chelan and because the economy is what it is, well, and you're assisting Detective Harris and…"

"We would love to have you in our little loop Mr. Woods. Is that what you;re trying to say?"

"Yes, that's what I was trying to say."

"Well, Chris and I had thought to ask you for help, but knew you were looking for a place to live and that it might be too much of an imposition."

"So you think it would clear with Chris and Detective Harris?"

"Yes, I believe it would. Like you said, the police department is down to a minimum of officers. I'm sure she would be glad for your help. Have you spoken to her?"

"Just this morning. She's good people. Did you know she was Pamunkey Indian?"

"No, I didn't. Never gave it any thought. Though we have a contingency of different natives right here in Chelan and throughout the state. We have people from just about every country in the world. I met a lady from Nepal two Sundays ago. How many people know there is a Nepal? Quite frankly, I didn't," Father commented, "or I had forgotten."

"I was trying to remember if you were the person that told me that George Tilden had asked about Brian Douglas."

"Yes, I did tell you that Mr. Tilden had asked about Brian a month or so ago. He's a building contractor. He said that he had talked to Brian concerning some kitchen work on one of the houses he owns."

"Who told me that Brian was a carpenter?"

"I believe I could have said that, or maybe Chris, or Mrs. Latham, the neighbor. I don't recall who else you talked to."

I wrote the names in my note pad. "It's my memory. I can't seem to rely on it totally. Now I'm trying to write everything down and then study it at home to see where I stand."

"When did you decide to go all in with us Stewart?"

This morning. I talked to my psychiatrist earlier this morning. She thought it was a good idea to get my mind busy. 'No loafing' is how she put it. It seems like the busier I am the better I operate. I also hired a trainer to get me in shape."

Father, what do you think about Mr. Tilden? How do you read him?" I asked.

"I don't know what to tell you. I only talked to him for a few minutes. About the only thing I remembered is that he referred to Brian in the past tense one time. Could have been an honest mistake."

"You mean like Brian was no longer with us."

Father nodded.

"So you're saying that Brian was a carpenter."

"Oh for sure, Brian was a master carpenter among other vocations. He was also an engineer, though not a lot of people around here knew that."

So I had a formal education. Carpentry was probably a hobby, I thought.

"How long has Brian been gone, Father?"

"Chris and I think it was sometime in October, I don't recall the exact date. I have it written down on my notes, which I didn't bring with me. Anyway, it was within days of Tom Workman's disappearance."

"Would that have been around October of 2011?"

He nodded.

That was over a year ago, I thought.

"That's a long time to be missing, and I gather that you and Chris just recently began looking for Mr. Douglas."

"That's right. I was aware that Brian was missing, but I felt like I was the only one who felt that way until Chris came to me with the same concern. Brian is a very private person. He disappeared once before with his government job and we just thought he might have gone off without saying anything, which was kind of his way," Father relayed.

So I was a loner, with few friends; probably not reclusive, but more to myself. Why not? I knew I had grown up an only child. I had to learn to do things by myself. My thoughts went back to Tom Workman. I knew from my startling realization at Mrs. Workman's house that Tom had fallen out of a plane. That' right!

"Father, who do you know that flies a plane?" I asked.

"You mean in the in the parish?"

"Ah, never mind Father. My question is so vague, please disregard." Father O'Reilly said he knew very little about George Tilden. I stood and the priest followed suit. I paid for the coffee and I returned Father O'Reilly to his home.

"Thanks for talking to me, Father, but now I've got to go."

"You're up to something, Stewart. Don't forget you're in the loop now?"

I made a turkey sausage sandwich, grabbed a stem of red seedless grapes and an Aloe Mango drink from the fridge. I sat at the table and picked up a book I had picked up at the Seattle Airport. It was an autobiography of the most lethal sniper in American military history. I had seen the man interviewed on one of the News channels and was interested in what a man that kills people is all about. Of course he was a good guy, a soldier, a family man. It's a very strange concept. Most of our lives are spent talking about never killing and once you're in the military, it's the reverse. Every military employee's job is directly or indirectly to kill the enemy. Some one tried to kill me and I really don't think I was the enemy, or was I? I wondered if I had spent time in the military.

Suddenly I heard a plane flying over the house. Apparently I was in one of the landing lanes. Oh my God. I put my sandwich down and looked for my cell phone. I checked the front room and finally found it on the kitchen counter.

"Hey Father I just realized something," I practically shouted.

"Is that important?"

"Yes, yes I think it is. I'll see you tomorrow."

I had called the priest earlier in the morning for a meeting and arrived at the restaurant that we had left the day before. As I entered the restaurant I could see that Chris Palmer was with him. They had waited to order breakfast. After eating and discussing the weather and every other topic, Father O asked me the question that was burning inside him.

CHAPTER EIGHTEEN

George Tilden, Bart Colangelo and Vandy Earhart were meeting in Tilden's building on the Avenue. Vandy had arrived early and gone directly to the conference room on the top floor. He was remembering when Bart had first talked to him about Brian Douglas.

Tom Workman discovered that Douglas was worth several millions of dollars. Douglas had no family living in Washington. He was almost positive that no one knew Douglas had this money, and had thought of a plan to get rid of Douglas where no one would ever find his body. The best part of Tom's plan had been that no one would have to kill the man. Vandy checked his watch. Where were Bart and George? He liked the idea of meeting here in Tilden's building on a Sunday. Vandy stood and walked to the door and just as he opened it, they were coming in.

"Going some where Vandy?" George chided.

"No, I was just going outside to wait."

"I told you we were going to get some refreshments and would be right back."

"All right. Sorry," Vandy replied.

"What do you drink with your Jack, Vandy?"

"I don't want a drink right now."

"Bart and I go all the way down to the liquor store and get a bottle of JB. Now you don't want a drink?"

"OK George I'll have a drink with water, coke or 7up."

George poured the drinks and sat a bowl of pretzels on the table. They touched glasses and took a drink.

"OK Vandy. What's got you all up in knots?"

"Well, first, you know that detective from Chelan that came to see you George?" He nodded.

"She's recruited four civilians and they're trying to find out what happened to Workman and Douglas."

"Civilians? Where did you pick that up?" Bart chimed in.

"Loretta Workman."

"I didn't know the police department could use lay people to do their job, George," Bart grumbled.

Vandy piped up, "It's in the news every night now; how every one's cutting back. Even the hospitals, firemen and the police departments have to cut back. Just like you too, right George?"

"Yeah, that's right. Everything is going to hell lately but there's not much we can do about it. Well, getting back to our problem. What have you heard?"

"You know that priest you talked to in Chelan."

George nodded.

"He and some woman whose name I don't know, have a new companion, but Loretta didn't get his name when he came to see her."

"Did he tell her why he came to see her?" George questioned.

"I don't know," Vandy replied.

"I think it was probably about her son," Bart offered, "the thing is Vandy we can't do anything about what is going on right now, except panic. We can sit around and speculate about what people are doing but we can't do a damned thing about it. If some one comes up to one of us and accuses us of murder, they have to have proof. They don't even have a body. It's been over a year and no one has said a word about Douglas or Tom. I still think we're in the clear. We've divided the money and no one has said anything about our spending habits, because we haven't done anything different. Are you worried about any of this so far George?"

"It has entered my mind on occasions. But no, I believe as you do Bart. About the only way that someone would corral us, would be if Tom or Douglas came walking out of the Mountains."

"There you have it Vandy. We have no control over what other people choose to do. Do you have something we can do about what's happening?"

"What you just said is pretty convincing Bart. Still, it just seems like there should be *something* we could do."

"Well Vandy," George responded, "if you come up with something we can do, call me."

They stood, clicked their glasses together and finished the drinks.

"I think I feel better, but I'm not sure," Vandy said from the door. "I'll see you guys."

"What do you think he did with his share of the money, Bart?"

"I don't know, George. Remember, we made a pact not to discuss what we would do with our share. Vandy's a smart man, I know he doesn't want to go to jail and he has a lot to loose. He's gong to be careful, just like you George. I know you don't want to go to jail."

"And you Bart?"

"Well George, I've always wanted a little place in Hawaii, nothing extravagant, just a place to go and sit in the sun, and drink a lot of beer, and do some snorkeling. A small villa in Italy would also be good. I'd like the to live in the southern part for a couple of months, where they drink real Italian wine and eat home style Italian food. I don't want to go to jail, so I'm going to do everything I can to keep from doing just that George."

"I appreciate Hawaii for a couple of weeks, but it has too much sun for me. I like the seasons. Some sun, and some snow on the slopes for skiing. I've always wanted to build a luxury hotel on the north side of Lake Chelan. Even have a big heated pool and a first rate restaurant at the top; something a person could take advantage of in the winter too. I have the money to make that happen now, but I'm going to sit on it for another year."

Bart nodded. "You know what's funny or maybe ironic, George? I really don't know you or Vandy, or for that matter, Tom Workman. Yet twelve or thirteen months ago we pulled off a big heist with very little preparation and to this day, no one knows a thing about it. No headlines. No one knows a thing. We're just going along like nothing ever happened. None of us has gone nuts with the money we stole. In the movies, someone always makes mistakes, or one of the characters gets greedy. Reckless spending or too much talking puts them in the big house. Don't you think this whole thing is ironic?"

"Yeah, and it sounds like you've given it a lot thought. So what *is your* story Bart?"

"Not much to tell. I'm an engineer who worked for Boeing for a few years, really didn't like the work, then my father died and left me a tidy sum of money. He had worked over at Rocky Reach Dam as a Civil Engineer. Dad was a man that loved what he did and tried to work at it seven days a week. You might say he lived to work. Me, I didn't have that kind of dedication or enthusiasm. Even when he would take time to vacation he was always working on whatever project he had going. I think the only reason he ever took time off was because mom would nag him. If she didn't, he would go years without any R&R. Any way, he died and my mother followed suit and I was their dotted on little prince. My father talked about how beautiful the Wenatchee Valley was and all of the fruit orchards that covered the landscape. The air is pure. This was laid back small town living. I fell in love with Wenatchee on my first visit. I paid too much for the orchard I bought in Orondo, but I'd do again. My wife hated the place and we split. She moved back to Seattle. I still see my daughter whenever I want and I'm happy. I like playing softball and basketball on the town teams and that's about it. In fact, that's where I met you, Tom and Vandy. I knew superficial stuff about each of you and I suppose that's all you knew about me. I know Vandy has a new tire business on the south end on Wenatchee Avenue, and that it has done well for him. I think he told me he had been married and is now divorced. I knew you were a businessman and that you had a building on North Wenatchee Avenue."

"Well Bart, you know about as much as me. I didn't even know that Tom Workman had worked for the Post Office. Vandy had put the OK stamp on him and I went along with it. I don't remember how I knew you owned an orchard, and until now I didn't know it was in Orondo.

I started out in Denver and visited Wenatchee some thirty years ago. I liked it because it had the Columbia River running through it and was small with plenty of space to grow. I didn't think it would ever grow fast because it has no industry here, except for Alcoa; nothing major to speak of though. I timed it pretty well because I was able to build some of the smaller strip centers here in Wenatchee and in Chelan. I even built some in Ephrata and Moses Lake. Now there are micro beer breweries, wine vineyards, boats of all kinds on the river and on Lake Chelan. We've grown to where a bigger prop plane is flying out of Pangborn field. I don't think a lot of the ole timers like it, but its just progress. Yeah, I love this area, especially Wenatchee and Chelan. I've gotten to the point where I think Leavenworth, Pashastin, Dryden, Waterville, Orondo, Cashmere will all be one place someday in the future. What do you think Bart?"

"I don't know George. When I think about all this it makes me think we're all good guys, gone wrong. Pretty sad don't you think?"

"For sure, but there's no turning back, Bart."

"Yeah, I guess not. I gotta go, George. Later."

CHAPTER NINETEEN

"All right Stewart, I've been holding back with this question all through breakfast. Why is it important that we know that George Tilden owns a plane?"

Christina and Father O were looking at me with anticipation. I had thought about this well into night and into the early morning and had slept very little because of it.

"If you had a friend, and this friend had a secret that could endanger your life because you had knowledge of it, would you still want to know the secret?"

" Would Father O'Reilly and I be in danger if you revealed this secret to us?"

"Yes, Chris."

"Is this secret about Brian Douglas?" Father O'Reilly asked.

"Yes."

Father O'Reilly asked, "Is the danger immediate?"

"It could be, depending on who finds out."

"Stewart, I for one will take that chance," Chris beamed.

"I'm with Chris, Stew."

God forgive me if I get these people killed or maimed because of my decision.

"I can't prove it but, I believe I'm Brian Douglas."

Chris gasped and Father O'Reilly shook his head.

"You don't look or sound like Brian," Chris said skeptically.

Father O'Reilly crossed his hands in front of him. "Why would you want to say something like that, Stewart?"

"I can only tell you what I know about myself from fourteen months ago. My accident robbed me of my long-term memory. This much I can tell you. I had the good fortune to remember my name three months after my misfortune."

I told them my complete story and when I finished, I could still see the doubt in their eyes. I didn't blame them. I'm not sure I would believe it. "

"So the manager at the hospital did a name search on Brian Douglas and found out where you had lived, and even where you banked?" Chris asked.

"Yes, yes that's right."

"So when you came to the church on our first meeting, that was just coincidental?"

"Yes, or maybe God's will, Father," I responded.

They smiled, but sat there at a loss for words.

"Fortunately, I had some very good doctors at the hospital and I'm told I will, in time, have some memory. It might be a hit and miss thing at first, but it will come back. I had my first flash of that memory at Mrs. Workman's home. I remembered Tom's face as he fell out of an airplane. As a matter of fact, I think it might be the very plane that Mr. Tilden owns. I put up a black board to keep tract of what I remember. George Tilden's name has been popping up and I want to find out more. I'm aware that I don't look or sound the same. When I made the decision to come here and find out what happened to me, I thought anonymity would be good. I could walk around and investigate without evoking suspicion, but because I still don't have complete memory it's very difficult. I was thrilled to find out I had friends in you and Chris. My worry was that if I told you who I was and it leaked out, your lives might be jeopardized.

"How would they find out, Stewart?

"Right this minute, I can't think of any way, but I'm sure there are ways; a slip of the tongue by one of you, or even by me. What my adversaries did to me has to be on their minds constantly, so their radar could pick up any little thing, even my presences here now. Though my plastic surgeon did guarantee me, I could walk into the lion's den and have dinner with them and never be found out."

"If you are Brian Douglas, I would agree with your doctor. I think I should believe that you are, because you're saying it. But my eyes say something different," Chris offered. "By the way, if you walked into your house would you recognize it?"

"I was given an address by Mrs. Mortensen in Seattle. Brian supposedly lived in Chelan. I don't know if I would know it now."

I wonder if you would be able to play the guitar. Brian knows how to play the electric guitar," Father O'Reilly said eagerly. "Do you have a key to your house?"

"I don't."

"How does a person have a key made without a duplicate key?" Father asked.

"You don't. You have to get a locksmith to put a new lock on your door," Chris informed.

"That's an interesting proposition, Father. I'm curious if my muscle memory is intact."

We pondered the question silently.

"I'm not trying to change the subject but I have two questions," Chris said quietly.

"Why are you here as an alias? And why can't you go to the police as Brian Douglas?"

"They're both good questions Chris. Well, in answer to your first one. Because I can move about easily here without those responsible for my accident knowing that I'm alive and back. They might want to make me disappear again. Originally I thought it might be better that the police didn't know that Stewart Woods was Brian Douglas, but I have since changed my mind. I believe that Detective Harris would be able to help us. I have a little different mindset now. All I want to do is find the people that did this to me."

"You have every right to feel that way. A whole fourteen months has been taken from your life," Chris expressed boldly.

"Thank you Chris. My friend Tom Wah Gee's nephew, Dr. Gee, speculated that I had been thrown out of a low flying plane; for the sole purpose of killing me. I've had a lot of time to think about who would do such a thing. I have considered every way a person can be killed and applied it to the killer or killers until…until, well,--- I felt like I was losing it. I stood and left the room, calmed myself and returned in less than a minute.

"What do you say we get back to finding out who did this to me?"

"Father, Stewart, what do think about this idea? Suppose I was to introduce you as my cousin, or uncle that has come to visit with the idea that you might live here someday?"

The men pondered the question.

"So you wouldn't appear to have just fallen out the sky," she added.

"Yeah, I get it. I'm here visiting. I wouldn't stand out, like I was here snooping around on my own. I'm your cousin and I get involved because of you. Yeah, I like it. What do you think, Father?"

"Yes," he nodded.

CHAPTER TWENTY

"Thank you for seeing me, Detective Harris. My name is Dane Creighton. I'm with the FBI, here to find out what happened to Brian Douglas. Brian worked in one of our affiliate bureaus. We like to think we take care of our own. I'm here to render my services. I prefer to work on my own, anything I find out I will certainly turn over to you. I would appreciate any information you might have on Brian Douglas, and if it at all possible I would like to remain anonymous."

"Whew, you really have a way about you, Agent Creighton. I feel like I've just be shaken down by a whirlwind and then set back down without knowing I had been shaken down, if you know what I mean."

"I think I understand Detective Harris. It's one of my shortcomings according to my immediate supervisor. I'm thorough but I talk to fast, like I'm trying to put something over on the person I'm talking to. Right?"

"We're simple people here Agent Creighton, but we manage to get by."

"I think I've put the wrong foot forward, Detective, I meant no offense. I'm originally from a small town in New Hampshire, population recently breaking eight hundred. Just a small town boy."

Harris looked at the baby-faced agent. Even in his suit he looked to be muscular, and at least six feet tall. He was heavier than her son who was also tall. He seemed sincere. So this is what an FBI agent looked like. The FBI agents she had seen on all those CSI programs were overbearing and had superior attitudes but this guy was a pussycat. She liked agent Creighton.

"I'm glad to have you aboard, Agent Creighton. So what can I do for you?"

"May I ask where you're from? You have a slight accent. One that I think I've heard before, in the east coast."

"You tell me," Detective Harris smiled.

"My first guess would've been North Carolina, but when you said, we're simple people here,' I knew it was Virginia, probably around Richmond somewhere."

I froze. I couldn't believe he would know that. How did he guess that? He was still looking at me anticipating my answer. He finally spoke.

"I've embarrassed you. Again I apologize," he said and sat back in his chair. He took a notepad from his valise. "Do you have the date Mr. Douglas disappeared and when you opened the file on him?"

"Did you know you would be talking to me before you arrived here today, agent Creighton?"

"No ma'am, I didn't. Accents are one of my hobbies; I spent time in Virginia, North Carolina and Massachusetts. I also visited the southern states along the Gulf of Mexico, including Georgia and Texas. Accents are a dying out, but you can still find them in the southern states. They're intriguing."

I was at a loss for words. As he looked at me I had the feeling he was aware he had spooked me. I reached for my file on Brian Douglas. I gave him all the information I had, which wasn't much, in just fifteen minutes.

"Are you staying here in Chelan?" I asked him as I put my file away.

"No ma'am, I'll give you my cell number. You can reach me anytime, and I would like to have yours."

He gave me a card. I looked at it.

"Just your name and telephone number."

"Yes, detective. I check in with my superior on a need basis, so it isn't necessary for you to concern yourself with me."

Was this arrogance or just the simple truth? I wondered.

"Do you have any other questions, Agent Creighton?"

"No ma'am, not at this time, but I'm sure some will come up as I gather information. Thank you for time and I hope I didn't offend you with my accent hobby."

"No offense taken."

As I sat at my desk thinking about what had just transpired, I was a little confused by Agent Creighton. I was thinking that I liked the young man, but at the same I had a strange feeling, and a wee bit confused.

CHAPTER TWENTY-ONE

Two days later I was at the airport checking on prices for flying lessons. I spent an hour and a half talking planes and signed up for the lessons I would need to fly a small aircraft.

Chris Palmer called me on my way home and wanted me to meet her at Heidi Latham's home.

"Thanks for meeting me here Stewart. Heidi is a little concerned about a man that was here recently," Chris told him as they walked up to the door.

"Come on in Chris, the doors open."

We sat at the kitchen table.

"I know I'm probably just blowing wind, but this guy that came here the other day has me worried. His name is Creighton, with the FBI. He was looking for Brian Douglas and wanted to know if I knew why he was missing, and was asking a bunch of questions, like he was someone important."

"He probably was important if he is with the FBI," I said.

"Said he was from Washington. I thought it might have something to do with the ATF. I think I told you that Brian had worked for the government, didn't I?"

I looked at Chris and she nodded, so I nodded. I was trying to figure out what he did for ATF.

Heidi spoke, "I just told him everything I had told you. He wanted to know if anyone had been in Brian's home since his disappearance. I told him I didn't know for sure. I hope I didn't say too much."

"I don't think you did, Mrs. Latham. You told Chris when you called her that he had asked about Stewart Woods by name?"

"Yes. He wanted to know who you were?"

I turned my eyes to Chris and she smiled.

"Stewart is my cousin, Mrs. Latham, and he had been interested in buying a home around here because I live here. It was just a coincidence that he stopped to look at Brian's house. Did the man ask about Tom Workman?"

"Oh yes. He wanted to know if there was anyone else missing. Told him where Loretta Workman lived, and he wrote it down."

"Anything else, Mrs. Latham?" I asked.

"Yes. How did he put it, Mrs. Latham? 'It would certainly make my job easier if you didn't say anything about me being here and talking to you. Could you do that for me?' That's what he said."

"I'm glad you told us," I said. "Have you told anyone else?"

"No, I told you, but I'm not telling anyone else."

"What do you think Stewart?" Chris asked from the side of her car.

"I was afraid of this. I knew if I came around here asking questions I might alert whoever is responsible. I thought my plastic surgery would keep me under cover. If I worked for ATF, he could be legit. Still, it could be someone that did this to Brian. By the way, why aren't you teaching school today?"

"Are you kidding, this is way more exciting. I'm on sabbatical for the next three months," she grinned.

"Would you like to come over to my place in Wenatchee for an hour or so. I've got to make a call. I'll fix you a salmon steak, green beans and a tossed salad."

"Ah, you remembered that you're a competent cook too."

"Yeah, I guess I am. Hey, I might even be able to play the guitar as Father O'Reilly, said." They laughed.

"It would be nice if you remembered me Brian," Chris said coyly.

"We were a twosome?"

"*I* thought we were." She blushed.

"Really. I was hoping we were more than just friends," Stewart mused.   "One of my weak points, I'm not very aggressive," she sighed.

"Do you like Stewart better than Brian?"

"I don't know Stewart yet. I did like Brian: he was gentle, soft spoken, reserved, and had a great sense of humor. Yes, I liked him a lot."

"I'm glad you said that. Well, we're here."

I parked in the garage, walked her through the whole house and told her I had to make a call. She sat in the front room. I walked to a bedroom and closed the door.

Approximately twenty minutes later, I opened the bedroom door and smelled the aroma of Salmon. When I got to the kitchen she was sitting with a glass of white wine, smiling. "Sorry I gabbed so long, Chris."

"It's all right, I hope you don't mind, but I beat you to the stove."

"It smells and looks great and I'm hungry." I rushed to her side and kissed her on the cheek. She blushed and stood. We kissed hard.

"I'm not *that* hungry," asI picked her up in my arms and walked into the bedroom.

Christina nudged me, "Hey Stewart, do you know it's almost four PM?"

CHAPTER TWENTY-TWO

As he drove to Pangborn Airport, George Johnson Tilden reflected on the day he driven home early and noticed a man come out his home in the distance. He had turned off into another long driveway until the stranger drove by. *Is my wife having an affair,* he wondered? He was unable to see the man clearly, but took notice of the car he was driving. George drove home and pretended he had seen nothing. When he asked her if anything exciting had happened that day. She responded that nothing of interest had happened, just a man looking for someone who had stopped earlier and she was unable to help. He knew better than to carry the conversation any further.

George was over six feet tall, with curly blonde hair and a ready smile, but he could be ruthless. His good looks had turned many a beautiful woman around for a second look. Men liked him because of his easy manner.

He remembered the first time he met Bart Colangelo and how outspoken he had been with George, calling Bart smooth, but dangerous. George had called, Rocky because he looked like Rocky Marciano and was even built like him. Bart wasn't afraid to say what he thought, and George liked people that were outspoken, even if it sometimes angered him.

George arrived at the airport and driven directly to the hangar that housed his plane. Three hangars over he could see two men talking and one looked like the person he had seen driving away from his home. Lately, George thought everyone looked like someone that was after him. All this paranoia was making him uneasy.

He took his Cessna out of the hangar and went through all the flight checks. The gas tank indicated three quarters full. The only thing he didn't do was to make a flight plan. He wanted to fly over the northwest Cascade Mountains toward the Canadian border. Those mountains were covered with snow year round.

The steady hum of the plane's twin engines was soothing and allowed him to think clearly. He was thinking of Loretta Workman. Would it do any good to offer her money, or would he have to deal with her disappearance? Should he wait for Vandy and Bart to discuss the situation? It was the first time he had done something like this that involved other people. Bart would probably be against any foul play and he was sure that Vandy would disapprove too. So it was up to him to do what he had to do. How would he lure her into his plane, or would he have to tranquilize her? Either way he would have to be very careful not to be seen. He had to make a plan. As he landed back on Pangborn Field, he was already thinking of the next thing he had to do. He had to find out if the person he saw coming out of his house was someone he had to be concerned about. How was he going to find that out? As he locked the hangar door, he realized what he must do.

As he Drove home his mind was still going back to Mrs. Workman, and something Bart had said before departing to Arizona. It was no ones fault Tom Workman had accidentally fallen out of his plane, and his only connection to Tom was his mother. She wasn't blabbing all over town, but other things were starting to happen. Even Bart had recently mentioned a new man in town had arrived.

The next morning George drove to Chelan to talk to the Catholic priest he had talked to a while back. He parked and was trying to think of the priest's first name when he saw a sign that indicated his name in front of the home he lived in.

The priest opened the door. "Ah, Mr. Tilden, " Father O'Reilly greeted.

"You have a good memory Father," George said as he followed the priest into the large front room.

"Your still looking for Brian Douglas?" the priest queried.

"That's right, I did hire a man but it didn't work out. I thought by now Brian might have shown up."

"No sir, not a word yet, but we have some people doing some snooping to find out what happened and where he might be."

"Oh so the police are finally involved. It's about time. Why hadn't they been involved from the start?" George asked.

"I think in a way it wasn't any one particular person's fault. The short staffing at the police department, because of the economy, plus the fact that no one had reported Brian missing until recently."

" I suppose you're referring to the Chelan police department," George ventured.

The priest thought about the question. "The Chelan police department is working on the Brian and Tom Workman's disappearance. I don't know if the Wenatchee police are also assisting on the case. Detective Marci Bush Harris from the Chelan department is the person we're working with."

"That's interesting," George nodded, "I wish I had the time to volunteer my assistance. How many are helping?"

"That would be great if you had the time. We have Detective Harris, Christina Palmer, Ms. Palmers cousin, Stewart Woods and myself."

" I'm surprised all of you have the time to do this extra work, Father."

"Well, it's not like we have the whole day every day to check around. I still have people I see during the day. I also make sick calls at the hospital and at private homes and do some counseling. But I still manage to get together with Chris Palmer and now with Stewart Woods at certain times. It is kind of a hit and miss thing. We don't have much yet, but then, we just got started. A thousand miles starts with the first step, Mr. Tilden."

"It sure does Father and you have a strong, positive attitude."

George Tilden left the priest's residence and drove home deep in thought. The whole situation was still pretty safe he guessed and no one would ever find a body. Not in those mountains. He wished Bart was still around so they could talk.. At least he had some names to watch out for now, Christina

Palmer and Stewart Woods. He wondered if Woods was the man Bart had referred to when he said there was a new man around.

As he drove down the long driveway toward his house, he saw a car parked in front of the fence that surrounded the ranch style home. Where do I know this car from? he wondered. He drove around to the back of the house, parked, and entered through the back door. He could hear Diane's laughter.

"Oh George, I'm glad you're home." The two stood when he entered. " Honey, remember when I told you that there had been a man here looking for someone, and I wasn't any help. This is the man. Stewart Woods, this is my husband George Tilden."

CHAPTER TWENTY-THREE

Stewart Woods had stopped at the small convenience store for bread, milk and orange juice, and as he slid back into the front seat he noticed a slip of paper on his windshield. He looked around to see if someone was watching, stepped out to fetch the note and quickly jumped back inside. He read the contents. It was from his friend, Cal with Turette's Syndrome. He drove home and called the number Cal had written on the note

"Thanks for calling me back, Mr. Stewart. That number I gave you is my work number, but I have my work phone with me all the time. I have two cell phones, one for work and one for funny business. I'm an electrician by trade, but can do almost anything. I have my own small electric company, with two additional electricians and manage to stay busy with Richardson Electric and so I'm all over the place, Chelan, Leavenworth, Dryden, Cashmere and Pashastin and all the small towns within a fifty-mile radius. There now you know almost all there is to know about Cal Richardson."

"You know Cal you didn't have to tell me all that. I believed I could trust you from the first time we met, although it's nice to know a good electrician. Did you have something to tell me?"

"I'm not sure it means anything, but there's a new man in town asking about Tom Workman and Brian Douglas. Says he's FBI. Again maybe I watch to many CSI programs, but I thought you should be aware. Maybe you already know."

"No, is there more?"

"I got this information from Loretta Workman yesterday. She couldn't remember everything he asked her, but he wrote every word down. She believed he was a real FBI man. Spent a whole hour and a half looking at pictures of Tom and asking some very personal questions. Maybe you should go and talk to Loretta, Mr. Woods. I'm not a good detective. She might remember more than I've been able to tell you."

"That's a good idea. I think I'll do just that. Hey Cal, be careful."

"I think I can trust Loretta Workman, Mr. Woods, but thanks for worrying about me."

"Loose lips sink ships, Cal. Remember that."

"Oh, Mr. Woods, I almost forgot to tell you about Loretta Workman. She's dating a man by the name of Bart Colangelo. The only thing I know about him is that he was a friend of Tom's. I'm happy for her because she is a nice lady and needs someone to lean on right now."

I thought about Mrs. Workman. She was an attractive lady and deserved someone nice. "That's interesting Cal, I hope it works out for her."

I reached across the seat and opened my note pad. I wrote down that Loretta Workman was dating a man by the name of Bart Colangelo and that I wanted to talk to her about the FBI agent.

CHAPTER TWENTY-FOUR

George Tilden stood at the door with his wife as Stewart Woods drove away.

"What did you think of Mr. Woods, George?"

"What was he doing here?" he asked calmly.

"He just came to tell me that he had found the man he was looking for and was now taking flying lessons at the airport. He wants to be able to fly around like you George."

"Is that what he said?"

"Now George, settle down. I'm the one that said that. I don't think I told him that you had your own plane." Diane thought for a few seconds. "I might have mentioned that you flew, I don't remember now whether I told him or not. It's not important George." She watched her husband as he stared at her. She could tell he was getting into one of his arguing moods. She didn't want to fight with him tonight. "I'm going to go visit Lillian. Do you want to come along?"

He walked off to the kitchen and she fetched her purse, "I've got my cell phone if you need me," she called from the doorway.

George poured a Scotch and water, sat in the front room and thought about Stewart Woods. One of his shortcomings was jumping to conclusions. Diane had always said that about him, and he knew it to be true. Was he putting to much emphasis on Woods? The man could be just who Diane said he was---a nice man. He had looked Woods directly in the eye when they shook hands and noticed nothing. Woods merely shook his hand and said that he was glad to meet him. There's nothing wrong with that picture. He smiled to himself and took a drink.

CHAPTER TWENTY-FIVE

My memory had been back for almost a week. I had waited to tell anyone, but now I was certain it would remain. I was anxious to tell Christina and Father O'Reilly. I called them and we met at Denny's on Wenatchee Avenue. I was really excited. I arrived early and waited in my car.

"My memory's back," I said, restraining my elation as we walked into the restaurant.

"For sure?" Chris beamed.

"A booth please," Father O'Reilly requested as we approached the counter.

"So tell us about it," Father requested after they had ordered coffee.

"I feel like some part of me just woke up and made me whole again. All this time with just partial memory made me awkward. Well, not about everything, Chris," I smiled sheepishly at her. She blushed, took a sip of coffee then, smiled at me. Father O'Reilly's eyes told me he understood. "I just woke up with a different outlook. I knew I was different from the minute my feet hit the floor. Somehow I knew it was my memory. I remembered winning the lottery with a ticket I bought in Seattle. I remembered going fishing with my dad at Coulee Dam. I remembered skipping school with Eddie Johnson and Tommy Michael and taking Eddy's father's Jeepster without consent and rolling it on Stimelt Hill, then lying about it till we couldn't." They listened intently. "I remember being pushed out of a plane."

"You folks ready to order some breakfast," the waitress asked.

We all ordered the same thing.

"I've had time to think about this. Father, Chris, I'm mad as hell and I'm going to get even. My life has been turned upside down by people I don't even know, and for what? Money. I know I should be dead, but by the grace of God, I live. I will avenge this nightmare I've been forced to live through." Impulsively I stood and walked to the bathroom, washed my face and peered at myself in the mirror. I was irritated by my outburst in front of the two people I respected most in this world. I do want to hunt down those who did this to me, but not at the cost of losing those I revere.

When I returned, our breakfast was on the table and they were working at it. They looked up when I sat. I picked up my fork, stirred my hash browns into the eggs and took a bite. *I had caused this silence.*

"I guess I sounded a little angry…and I am, but when I find them, I'm not going to lynch them from the nearest tree." I looked at Father O'Reilly and saw a question in his eyes. "Do you want to talk about it Father?" I asked.

He sat back. "I'm not sure it's any of my business, Brian. No I guess I don't want to talk about it."

Chris interjected. "I think I know what Father wants to ask you, because I have the same question nagging me. I think I know you well enough to ask and not feel like I'm prying, Brian. Would you tell us about the winning lottery ticket you bought in Seattle?"

These are my closest friends and I felt bad for not telling them I now was very rich.

"I should have told you sooner, but really, your safety took precedence. However now that we've been working together and if and if any of the bad people are aware of it, it probably doesn't matter. They would probably assume I have told you the whole story by now."

Okay, better late than never. I'd gone to Seattle to purchase a couple of special tools for my carpentry. I'm sure my story is quite ordinary on the purchase of a lottery ticket. After buying my tools I went next door and bought a bottle of 7up in a 7-11. The store was quiet and the owner and I just made small talk. I discovered that his sister lived in Chelan. He was aware that Chelan was a small town and asked me if I knew Loretta Workman. I told him I didn't. About that time a customer came in and wanted to buy 20 dollars of quick picks, you know the lottery ticket thing. The owner punched out two tickets of ten picks and the man searched his pockets for the twenty dollars he thought he had. The man left talking to himself. I asked him how much the lottery was worth. At that time it was twenty million. I liked the owner, offered to buy the twenty tickets and the rest is history. He asked me for my name and I told him. Honestly, I never gave it a thought that I might win. I bought the tickets because the man was nice and polite plus his sister lived in Chelan. The truth is I had forgotten I even had the tickets until I read in the paper that the winner hadn't come forward with the winning numbers. The tickets had sat on my dresser for almost two months before I picked them up to look at them."

Chris asked, "How much was it when you won?"

"Thirty six million."

Father O'Reilly shook his head, and uttered, "thirty-six million."

Christina just stared with her hands to her mouth.

"Well, I took a one payment lump sum and after taxes I only received a little over eighteen million."

"Did it ever enter your mind that," and Christina paused, "that someone might want to abduct you for those millions?"

"It did. If I hadn't stopped at that 7/11 for a cold 7up and everything that transpired as it did at that time, I would never have disappeared and gone through all I did. Am I happier for having won all this money? Yes…and no. Circumstances had me buying a lottery ticket once before. I didn't win. I didn't expect to win. The truth is money can be evil. I thought I had done everything to keep from anyone knowing I had won all these millions. I had innocently given my name and telephone number to the 7/11 owner, whose sister lived in Chelan. Steve Wilson, the owner had wanted my number to give to his sister because she had wanted a porch built over her back door. I even opened a bank account in Seattle so no one in Chelan would know anything about my good luck, but as time moved on I thought of things this money could do. I was quite dismayed by our veterans who were coming home without legs and arms. I contacted the Wounded Warrior Foundation and discovered three local veterans needed help.   One of the first things I did with the money was to purchase a home for a Navy veteran. Mary Esther Lopez had gone to Chelan High School. She had joined the Navy and became a Corpsman. She was stationed with Ist Marine Division out of Camp Pendelton. Later she shipped out with her Marine Corps unit to Iraq. Her unit had been in several confrontations with Al Quada and Mary had received two Purple Hearts and the third highest medal, the Silver Star for valor. She spent three deployments in Iraq and in the last one, she lost a leg up to just above the knee and part of her other foot. She spent the last year of her six-year hitch at Johns Hopkins Hospital learning to walk on a metal leg and foot.

Brian Douglas had purchased the home she was proudly living in now. I had recently visited her as Stewart Woods.

"Where is Brian Douglas, Mr. Woods? I haven't seen him in months. So you're a good friend of his. Come in and I'll show you all the things that Brian did to make it possible for me to live here. He was a remarkable carpenter. On the stairs he designed two rails that run from the bottom of the stairs to the top. Though I've become so proficient on my leg and foot, I only need one of the rails. At the back door, for the three steps leading to the ground, he put rails made of some kind of special treated wood that won't rot." She led him to the bathroom. "Here he made the bathroom with an adjustable chair where I can sit and shower. He thought of everything. He even designed the gas pedal of the Ford Focus that I drive. He told me I was his heroine, but really, he is my hero.

"How well do you know Brian Mr. Woods?"

I looked into her deep brown eyes. "As well as I've known anyone in my life. I was aware he was a fine carpenter. Does the bathroom chair have any problems?"

"No, everything works perfectly. Are you also a carpenter, Mr. Woods?"

I smiled trying to cover my mistake. "I'm not Brian Douglas good, but I do a little carpentry."

"It's funny but Brian said that the chair in the first floor might give me some problem when he put it in, but it still works well. Would you like a beer Mr. Woods?"

She led me to the kitchen and brought us two Heinekens in the bottles. I watched as she moved around on her leg and foot flawlessly. She had adjusted so well and was still a beautiful lady. I don't think I ever heard her say anything negative about her missing limbs. *A real warrior,* I thought.

"I live with my mother and a younger brother. I'd heard that The Wounded Warrior Foundation was helping military people that came back with missing limbs, and PTS. Someone purchased this home and then donated it to me. This home once belonged to George Tilden, a long time house builder in Wenatchee. I worked for Mr. Tilden, briefly, as a secretary.

That's right. Tilden had owned this house, but I hadn't purchased it directly from him. I had bought it from a couple that lived in the house for less than a year. The couple did not like Wenatchee and moved back to Everett. So Mary had worked for Tilden, briefly; wonder why she quit?

"Where is Brian Douglas Mr. Woods?"

"That's the 64 thousand dollar question, Mary. Where is Brian Douglas? No one knows where my friend is, but I'm confident he is alive and doing well, whereever he is."

"Have you spoken to the other two recipients of homes in the area. One lives in Leavenworth and the other in Tonasket. Maybe one of them heard from him. Brian did the same things to their homes. I have their addresses, if you need them."

"Thanks Mary, I appreciate that."

She walked away and returned with the addresses.

"Oops, I didn't know Mary had a guest," her brother said, as he entered the kitchen.

"I was just leaving."

"This is my brother Roberto, Mr. Woods." We shook hands and I left.

As I drove away I felt devious, but knew it was for the best. I would eventually tell Mary who I really was, but not now.

On the way home I decided I would enter the lion's den, since I was completely unknown and see what I could find out. As soon as I arrived home, I went to the spare bedroom and checked my notes on what I had learned so far. I wrote down that my memory was back, dated it, and drew a black line across the paper as a cut off from when I was speculating. I knew for sure it was George Tilden who had flown the plane. I was almost certain I had never spoken to Tilden, which begged a different question. How did Tilden know I had money? Now my brain was clicking. I was almost certain I had never told anyone. I wondered about Tom Workman. Did he fall or was he ejected like me? There was a lot of turbulence at that time. I played it back in my mind. The picture that Mrs. Workman had shown me of her son, Tom, is what started my memory working. *The mind is a strange thing.* I entered the kitchen and grabbed a beer. I was the fool. Workman obviously knew George Tilden and those other goons who I still don't know. My problem was breaking into the small clique. However, I was now invisible. I finished my beer and moved to the front room. I hated this moat I was wallowing in. I turned the TV on, channel surfed for a few minutes, found nothing of interest, and turned it off, went into the bedroom and lay down. My brain was running at a hundred miles an hour. I was about to look for something to eat when the doorbell rang.

"I hope I haven't come at a bad time," Christina said timidly.

"I've never been happier to see anyone as I am at this very moment."

"Is everything all right?"

"It is now. Come in."

I lead her into the kitchen. "Have you eaten dinner?"

"No."

"Good. May I fix you a salmon steak with broccoli, whole corn and a tossed Caesar salad?"

"Umm, sounds good. Will you be joining me?"

"I sure will." I opened a bottle of red wine and poured us each a glass and then began fixing the dinner."

"I'm delighted that you're glad to see me Brian. I wasn't sure I should just drop in on you, and may I call you Brian?"

"Only if you can remember to call me Stewart out in public."

No more than ten minutes had passed when Brian brought the food to the table.

"Wow, that was fast and it smells delicious Brian. I was hungry and didn't realize it."

"How was school today?"

"I've got some really good students this year. There always seems to be a barnacle in each classroom, but this year I don't have any. School is great. What kind of student were you?"

"I'd be blowing my own horn. I was an attentive student. I liked school in every respect. I think my being an only child gave me some advantages. I had to find things to do on my own, for one, and then I didn't have anyone to socialize with so I did a lot reading. My parents were both professional people, and that helped immensely. I did well in school."

"I thought you might have been a better than average pupil. Did you have a good day?"

"I did. Christina I never told you about myself because I'm naturally an introspective person. It doesn't mean I don't trust you, or that I don't want to tell you things. I know I need to work on being more open with you and Father O'Reilly. Before you arrived today I was suffering from suffocation of my own doing and you arrived at just the right time to rescue me. I really need you to be around."

Christina got up from the table and came over to me looked into my eyes, and we kissed passionately.

"Whew, would you like a refill on your wine?"

"I don't think I need any more wine."

"Nor do I."

CHAPTER TWENTY-SIX

Keep you friends close and your enemies closer, came to mind. Cliché's were not my thing, but that one nagged at me. It had been around eighteen months since I had been abducted. My relationship with Christina Palmer had diverted me from my pursuit of those responsible, however the onus was on me. I was happy and only occasionally thought of my problem. I had learned to fly an airplane and then helped Christina learn to fly. Christina's infatuation with the beauty of Catholic churches had convinced her to become a Catholic. I had actually tried to discourage her from doing so, but in the end she became an "idol worshiper". I say that with a smile. A friend of mine, who happened to be a Baptist, once asked me if we indeed, prayed to all the statues in Catholic churches. I wasn't sure I could explain all the figures that adorned our churches. They had always been there and I just never questioned them; tougher than that was the question of asking a priest to forgive you for all your sins. Faith: was my stock answer.

Anyhow, my life had managed to move along on a happy path until I read in the Wenatchee World that Caldwell Richardson's body had been pulled out of the Columbia River. I read the article about my friend's unfortunate accident, which the paper said was what officials presumed it was. Cal had been fishing on his boat, and somehow fallen overboard and drowned. No foul play was attributed to his death. The paper made notice that Cal had Turret's Syndrome and that one of the tics might have prompted his fall. It had been months since I had talked to Cal. He wasn't your average guy, but he had a big heart. I reread the column and then tried to put the man out of my mind.

I arrived at Christina's home a little after five in the afternoon. We went to Andante Restaurant, just off Woodin Avenue, in Chelan.

We ordered two large Caesar salads and white wine.

"All right Stewart, what's bothering you?"

I stared at Christina.

"Hey, you've been moping around ever since you arrived. Talk to me, please. Remember the guy that said he would be a little more open to me and Father O'Reilly."

"I said that?"

Chris reached across the table and held my hand.

"No it was that other guy whose name I can't use in public."

"Did you know Caldwell Richardson?"

Chris shook her head. "I read the article this morning because he did come to my house a couple of years ago to fix my furnace. He definitely knew in his business. He did bark a couple of times in my presence but treated it no different than a cough; it was so much of his life, he assumed you understood. No I didn't know him; not really. How well did you know him?"

"He approached me when I first got back from Seattle after my accident. He was a strange man. You know, he thought I might be Brian Douglas until he found my picture in an old newspaper in the library. I didn't get to know him as a person. I liked him though. His best friend was Tom Workman, and he really wanted to know what happened to him."

"Why in the world would he think you were Brian Douglas?" Chris asked.

"He had noticed that I was snooping around with you and Father O'Reilly and that he hadn't seen me around before. Plus he didn't know what Brian Douglas looked like until he checked it out in old newspapers at the Daily World." I smiled, "He was a CSI guy and loved those detective stories on T.V., but never thought he would make a good policeman. You know Chris, I think I'll check with Detective Harris tomorrow and find out the particulars on his drowning."

"Do you think he might have been killed?"

"I don't know but I'm going to check it out."

Detective Harris referred me to Detective Don Jones in Wenatchee. The drive to the Wenatchee Police Department had me changing my mind almost every block until I arrived. Even then I sat in my car until I saw the meter man coming down my side of the street. I got out and put fifty cents in the meter.

"I'm here to see Detective Donald R. Jones. My name is Stewart Woods," I said to the desk officer.

"All right Mr. Woods. Have a seat and he'll be with you a few minutes."

I sat, took out my note pad, and started to call Chris when a man came out of an office. I recognized the face, but not the name. I knew this man. I stood and as he walked by me. I wasn't sure I should say anything? He reached the door to the street and I spit out his name.

"Agent Creighton?"

He turned, walked back to me, and looked at me carefully. "Do I know you sir?"

"The detective is ready for you Mr. Woods," the desk officer told me.

"Yes…yes, I'll be right there," I stuttered, Ah… could I have your card with a number I can reach you?"

Creighton pulled out a card and handed it to me.

"I have an appointment with Detective Jones, but I'll call you soon, Agent Creighton."

He turned and walked out the door.

Detective Jones ushered me into his office.

"So you know agent Creighton, Mr. Woods?"

"I, I met him a few years ago in D.C. and remembered him. It surprised me to see him here. In fact, I was shocked I remembered his name," I smiled nervously.

We sat down.

Detective Jones observed me curiously. "Did you work for the FBI, Mr. Woods?"

I didn't want to go there. "No," and hoped it would stop at that.

"As I told you on the phone, I really don't have much to add about Mr. Richardson. There's nothing to indicate there was foul play. He was well known around the county. No enemies. I suppose you knew he was afflicted with Tourette's. It might have played a part in his falling over board, but it's only speculation. It is not my belief, but one of his employee's had suggested it. There is absolutely nothing to suggest he was murdered, except he wasn't wearing a life vest. But then, some times people just forget to put them on."

I walked out of the station and looked around for agent Creighton. I was almost certain he would be close by, waiting for me. I stood by my car and kept looking for him to show. After a few minutes I sat in my car. *Maybe Creighton had an appointment somewhere else,* I thought. I didn't have any place special to be but I didn't want to just sit here in my car. I saw someone running back to the station and recognized Creighton. "Hey Dane!" I yelled and he hurried across the street toward me.

He stood a few feet from me and checked me up and down. "I'm pretty sure I don't know you, but I'm dying to know how you know me. I'm a long way from home and certainly didn't expect anyone to recognize me in this little town."

"There's a good reason for that Dane," and I proceeded to briefly tell him a long story in two minutes.

He still had doubts as he had listened intently.

"What do you know about me?" He asked.

"You're an FBI agent from a little town in New Hampshire and you also play a mean guitar. I met you at a conference at the Mayflower Hotel in D. C."

Dane smiled, "Who was the chick that was staying there that we laughed about one evening?"

"Well, we made fun of a lot of people, but I think you're referring to Anna Vesuvius."

"Brian your own mother probably didn't recognize you," Dane laughed.

I talked Dane into following me home and we talked for hours about everything. He then mentioned he would be going back to D.C. in the morning and that he had to tell me all he had discovered in his four days here in Wenatchee.

"I'll give you all I have on your disappearance, with some names of 'persons of interest.' The reason you saw me at Detective Jones office is because he was the investigating officer of the Caldwell Richardson drowning. Personally, even though there isn't enough conclusive evidence, I think someone pushed Richardson overboard. He called me after he saw me at Loretta

Workman's home. Incidentally, he mentioned he had talked to you, referring to you as Stewart Woods."

"Yeah, we did talk. I didn't want to tell him who I really was for fear of jeopardizing his life, and looked what happened anyway. That was my motive for talking to Detective Jones."

Dane retrieved his notepad from the car and showed Brian the names he had accumulated.

"Well, some of them I don't recognize, but I know these four."

"Look Brian, Bill Tilden is definitely a person I would want to talk to because he has motive. He's a commercial builder and is in some financial difficulty of late. I was going to give these names to Detective Harris in Chelan, but I suppose you can relay them to her for me and check them out yourself. I believe some of these men are minions, or at least collaborators of Tilden. I certainly would do some snooping on them. I did get a chance to talk to a guy by the name of Colangelo. That's another guy you definitely need to talk to. He and Tilden are good friends, though Tilden denied that when I interviewed him. You'll see that in my notes. This little gang all played softball together in the town's summer leagues. Another thing, there's a young woman who worked for Tilden as receptionist that I didn't get chance to interview. She lives in Leavenworth. Anyway, they had an affair and he had to fire her. That left some bad feelings from her. She might be able to give you some stuff that Tilden wouldn't want you to know. Her name is Betty Tillums. She preceded the girl he has there now and she's only been there a few months." Creighton stopped talking and studied me curiously. "So no one knows Brian is in town trying to find the bastards that tried to kill him, Stewart?"

"Hey Dane. What's that supposed to mean?"

"Does Detective Harris know that Stewart Woods is Brian Douglas?" Brian asked with a smirk on his face.

"I'm not going to lie to you. I think it's best that she not know for the time being. Father Damon O'Reilly and Christina Palmer know that I'm Brian Douglas."

"How long did you say you had been out of commission?"

Dane was just being an FBI agent right now, and I knew he was my friend no matter what I was doing. I stood, walked to my front window, and stared out for few minutes.

"I was down for almost fifteen months. I had six major broken bones. My face had been erased clean like a black board. I lost twenty five per cent of my body weight and my psyche was butchered into Taco filling. I still have trouble focusing with both eyes. I only recently got my memory back. I'm still taking blood thinners to keep from having a stroke or heart attack. I think I was always a good Catholic boy and thought good things most of the time. Well, that has changed. I don't know to what degree it will carry me, but I plan on finding out who did this to me and I will..." I was on the verge of losing my dignity so I stopped talking. I felt the squeeze of his hand on my shoulder and then the front door opened and closed.

The next morning I was at the airport at four thirty. Dane came walking in, smiling as he greeted me.

"I knew you'd be here this morning, Stewart."

We made small talk for a few minutes and then he wanted to check in early because he had to call someone and discuss a problem that faced him in D.C.

He whispered to me as we hugged, "I'm not a good Catholic boy, so when you're ready to do what you're going to do Brian, call me and I'll help you."

Our eyes locked for a few seconds, then he turned and entered the check in line.

CHAPTER TWENTY-SEVEN

I had been observing Vanderbilt Earhart's movements, from a distance for the past week and as I reminisced the police file Detective Harris had obtained for me, Earhart drove into the north end of the Safeway parking lot on Wenatchee Avenue.

Vanderbilt 'Vandy' Earhart's father had died a fairly young man and Vandy's mother had married a man that abused alcohol. At age twelve, he became his stepfather's punching bag. Vandy became withdrawn and hostile. It didn't take long for him to start hanging out with the wrong crowd at school when he did attend. He wouldn't come home some nights, which would exacerbate his problems with his stepfather. He eventually was sent to a reform school in Chehalis, Washington. When he was released at eighteen, he came back to Wenatchee and with a promise to behave, his uncle, Robert Earhart, brother of his real father, offered him a job at his tire shop. He managed to learn his uncle's business and wanted to have his own tire shop. One of his old hang out buddies talked him into robbing a bank in Seattle. Vandy knew it was risky but he thought he could then open his own business in tires. A bank guard was killed. They were caught; he spent eight years in Walla Walla state prison, and then returned to his uncles business. His uncle hired him back because Vandy's motive for wanting the money was to build his own tire store. His uncle noticed that prison life had changed Vandy into an angry, friendless young man, his temper easily evoked. Vandy held his uncle in high veneration and demonstrated total respect for the quiet businessman. In return, his uncle never criticized his nephew and allowed him to make mistakes without lecturing.

I parked three cars down from Earhart's red Ford Mustang and watched him walk to the Safeway store. I waited for five seconds, then left my car. I looked around to see if anyone was watching me as I walked to the Mustang and placed the note on Earhart's windshield, then went back to my car. I drove across the avenue two blocks away and parked where I could see his car. I took my binoculars from the glove department and focused on the Safeway entrance until I saw him exit and walk to his car. He placed his purchase behind the drivers seat and got into his car, then immediately jumped out, and quickly looked around. He appeared to be upset because he pounded the top of his Mustang. Even with my binoculars I couldn't tell if he was using his cell phone while he was parked. After a few minutes, he drove down Wenatchee Avenue. I waited until he was well down the avenue before I began following him. Vanderbilt had picked the perfect car to follow: red. I hit a red light but I could still see him driving north on the avenue. *In a hurry red lights always seem to take longer to change,* I thought. I had lost the red car. I drove slowly on the slow lane and checked both sides of the street. I spotted his car in Tilden's Commercial Building Enterprise parking lot. I kept driving north and turned left at Blossom Avenue, drove into Walmart's lot and parked.

    Creighton had pretty much summarized the small group of names he had gathered. At least Earhart and Tilden. There did seem to be some connection. Coincidence? I shook my head slowly. I was thinking about how to approach Earhart when I caught a red Mustang drive into the parking lot in my rear view mirror, at least it appeared to be a Mustang. The sun's rays were shining down on the car's window and blinding me. I couldn't even distinguish the driver. It was moving toward where I was parked. Had I been made? I could feel the sweat forming under my armpits and felt warm all over. When it was less the thirty feet from me…it stopped. *This guy has done time in Walla Walla.* I thought. I stopped looking in my rear view mirror and waited. I was trying to think of what I would say to him when he finally reached my car. I was looking straight ahead, waiting for the car to appear. I was sure I looked sweaty and guilty.

CHAPTER TWENTY EIGHT

    I was in some form of vehicle and could hear talking and laughing. I was dizzy and a little nauseous. It bothered me that I couldn't remember taking anything that would do this to me. Intuitively I knew this was not a car or train. I rolled back and forth and my body banged against a wall or siding. Suddenly I felt a cold breeze strike my face. Again there were voices and I felt hands tugging, pulling, and lifting. My chest hit something hard. A rush of cold air slapped my face. A face came into view and I smiled at it. He was looking at me and talking, but I couldn't understand what he was saying. Now I realized I was in a plane---and then I wasn't. I felt a sense of lightness and was having trouble focusing my eyes as the tops of the green trees that were getting closer every second. Instinctively, I tried to open my arms, to no avail. My body was bound by something. I could see a white covering rushing up to meet me and I realized I was going to "aaaahhhh," I screamed and sat straight up in bed. The room was dark except for the red numbers on my digital clock on the bed stand. It was 3:12 in the morning. I was panting hard and could hear my heart thumping. Was I near death? That scared me because I thought I might be having a heart attack or at least something serious. I threw the covers off and dropped my feet to the floor, reached over and turned the lamp on. I was about to stand when I thought I heard a door close. I froze and listened. I had stopped breathing and felt dizzy again. I let out the trapped air in my lungs slowly and took in a new breath. "You had a bad dream and that's all, Brian. Now get your butt up and go wash your face," I said out loud. It was my whistling in the dark routine. I stood unsteadily and shuffled slowly into the bathroom. Clicking on the light, I stood in front of the mirror stared at the nearest thing to Casper the ghost, I had ever seen. My face looked oily and moist, with dark bags under my eyes, little red lines in the white of my blue eyes. I really looked like...well, I was glad that Christina wasn't here to see this face. I washed my puss with soap, combed my hair; checked the front door. It was locked. *Maybe it wasn't a door I heard*, I thought. *What else could it have been?*

CHAPTER TWENTY-NINE

I had invited Christina and Father O'Reilly over to finally explain how I thought my abduction had its beginning. I barbequed steaks and baked potatoes for our dinner. I had wine and beer and after a couple of glasses we had labored discussions on the Apple Blossom Festival and the new Sports Center.

"Brian, are you having second thoughts about telling us about your ordeal?" Christina asked hesitantly.

"I guess I have been avoiding the whole thing. Dr. Lansing said I might do this subconsciously because I was afraid to face it."

We finished dinner, were on our second bottle of red wine, and still sitting at the kitchen table. I got up and made a fresh pot of coffee. Christina and Father O'Reilly sat waiting patiently.

"The purchase of the lottery ticket that won me all the money was quite by chance," I said leaning against the kitchen counter." The reason I bought the tickets was because I had befriended the storeowner. A man had come in, ordered twenty tickets and then couldn't find the money to pay for them. He left grumbling to himself about the money he thought he had brought."

"How did you happen to be in the 7/11 in the first place? Christina asked.

I nodded, "Yes…I had gone to Seattle to pick up some special carpentry tools at a place called, 'From Floor to Roof.' They carry all kind of tools for house building. They're the Dick's Sports Shop of the building trade. Anyway, I got my tools and the 7/11 was next door, so I went in to get a 7up for my drive back to Chelan."

"You drove a hundred and fifty miles to buy some tools for your hobby?" Father asked.

"Yeah, that's what I did. It had been a couple of years since I'd been there and I was looking at some of the new tools that had arrived since my last visit. I looked down at the last gasps of the percolating coffee pot, pulled the plug, and brought the pot to the table. I poured myself another glass of wine and drank it down. I was aware that I had their attention and that the wine was making me less inhibited.

"I suppose, because his business was quiet at the time, and because his sister lived in Chelan, I was compelled to buy the tickets that the man had requested, but was unable to buy. I plunked twenty dollars on the counter where we had been chatting. He insisted that I didn't have to buy the tickets, but I picked up the two ten dollar slips, and had started for the door, when he asked me for a business card, and he gave me his. He said his sister wanted a porch built over her back door. I gave him my card and thought I would never hear from him again or his sister. I put the tickets over the sun visor in my car and forgot about them. I didn't use the sun visor until I had been back to Chelan a couple of weeks. When I pulled the visor down, out fell the two ten dollar tickets on my lap. I had forgot about them. Later, I took them into my house and laid them on my dresser, where again, I forgot about them.

The Washington Lottery Board was looking for the person or persons who had won the 36 million dollar prize in a previous drawing. The caption in the Wenatchee World newspaper also stated that the winner or winners should come forward or it would be added to some future drawing. The winning numbers were printed across the bottom of the article.

"Only then did I go to my dresser, compared the numbers and discovered that I had won. I freaked out. I was so happy and at the same time I was sad. I wanted to tell you Father. I didn't know you very well then Chris." Suddenly I felt ill. "Father, Chris excuse me but I think I'm going to be sick." I rushed off to the bathroom; threw up the dinner and turned white: *Too much wine?* I was reliving that day again, and for the same reasons.

I finished throwing up and sat on the throne until I heard a soft knock on the bathroom door.

"Brian, are you all right in there?" Chris asked in hushed voice.

"I'll brush my teeth and be there in a minute," I responded weakly.

"Did you take some Pepto Bismol? she asked

"That's the pink stuff right?"

"Yes."

"Yeah, and I already feel better. How long have I been in here?'

"A little over fifteen minutes," Chris responded.

Father O'Reilly and Christina had cleared the table and moved to the front room.

"I apologize..."

"Maybe we should let you collect yourself and..."

"No, please, no, let me finish telling you the whole thing. Please! I'm all right now. I want you to know everything."

"You sure you want to continue?" Chris asked.

"Yes, let me talk it out. I think that's what Dr. Lansing said. I've got to do it. I've been avoiding this too long.

Where was I?"

Father spoke up. "You were happy and sad about winning all the money."

I nodded. "I'm not going to say I wasn't happy about winning the money. I was very happy. The thing is, I've never really wanted much. I was happy with the way my life was going. I've read what has happened to people who win millions or who come into great fortunes. Their lives do change, mostly for the worse. Sure I'd like all the new gadgets for my hobby, and I suppose I could get a new car. Do I need any of it? I don't think so. I don't know if you recall anything about Sam Walton, the founder of Wal-Mart Stores. He was one of the few men who never changed his life after he became a millionaire, and eventually a billionaire. One of the stories I read or heard about the man was truly remarkable. He lived in the same house most of his life and when a reporter went to his home to interview him, He wrote that the furniture was not new and displayed wear. The couch that the reporter sat in was frayed on the edges, and his hunting dogs were allowed in the home. Mr. Walton still stood in line in Rogers, Arkansas for his duck tags along with the other duck hunters in his hometown. He was just another citizen. Sam Walton was my hero because he remained who he was despite all the hoopla. He loved his wife and changed very little in his lifestyle." I paused.

"What about all the charities and the Heart and Cancer foundations, Leukemia, Parkinson's Disease, Alzheimer and Dementia? Couldn't you donate to those places?" Chris asked. Father nodded to the suggestion.

"I certainly considered those very things along with donating to a Wounded Warrior Project, through which I did sponsor two individuals in our area. The foundation is primarily for returning military people with missing limbs and mental stress problems from the wars. I had thought I would study each foundation and when I had an interest, send a check with a request for complete anonymity. It worked fine for the two military people I sponsored and then I was abducted. I thought I had been very careful about keeping this lotto thing a secret. It had been over a year since I won the money and no one knew it, at least I didn't think anyone knew. I had purposely opened an account in Seattle where I had purchased the ticket and deposited the biggest share of the 19 million after taxes in that bank." I stopped talking and walked out of the room. In less than three minutes I returned with a carry on suitcase and set it on the floor.

"How much money do you think I can put in this bag that fits in an airplane overhead compartment, Father, Chris?"

They both stared at the bag.

"Wouldn't it depend on the denominations of the bills?" Chris responded. Father nodded in agreement.

"Good. That's right. My confidant at the bank told me off the top of his head that a million dollars weighs approximately 20 pounds, in 100.00 dollar bills."

"Are you saying you brought 2 million dollars in a 40 pound carry on case back to Chelan from Seattle?" Chris asked dumbfounded.

"No I was just pointing out that 2 million dollars fits into a 40 pound bag."

"Why?" Father O'Reilly asked puzzled.

"Earlier when I told you that money changes people. I'd never had that much money and as the reality of it came down on me, I started doing strange things. Why you ask? Honestly I don't know what I was thinking when all this popped into my brain. Telling you two had been an option, but I talked myself out of it. I suppose *we* could have come up with some solution with what to do with all this money, but it just wasn't there in my head to do it. The money overwhelmed me with its mere presence. It was doing what I had supposed it does to most people, though I never felt like I was most people. I thought I was beyond all this craziness, but I spent many sleepless nights conjuring all that I could do with this money and then in the morning…have a complete change of mind. Instant millions of dollars has a personality that easily manipulates the soundest of minds. Even though it doesn't utter words it has a voice like no other. Everything seems possible. There is nothing I didn't think of and its power kept me confused, afraid and reclusive. I guess I sound like a raving maniac. Most of the time I could forget about the money, but it doesn't go away: it dictates your life." Again I paused. "The only person that knew I had purchased a lottery ticket was the man that owned the 7/11 in Seattle. I had given him my card. That's right. Oh my God, I laughed. I did call the man about how to collect the money from the ticket I had. In my frenzy about winning I had called him and told him I had won with the tickets I bought from him. I was the leak!! I can't believe I was so dumb."

"Why would you want to call him?" Father asked.

"I thought he might know how to redeem the ticket."

"Would that be Loretta's brother? Chris asked.

"Right. The funny thing is I can't remember if we ever introduced ourselves. We just talked because there wasn't anyone else in his store."

"Is it important that you know his name?" Father asked.

"I think you said you had given him your business card."

I thought for a few seconds. "Yes, you're right."

"Did Loretta Workman ever call you about putting a porch over her back door?"

"No she didn't."

Father spoke, "Do you think the owner of the 7/11 relayed your name and address to Loretta Workman?"

"I don't know, I guess it's possible."

"What about the guy at the bank?" Chris asked.

"Yeah, I guess that's possible too. I dealt directly with the president. He thought it was better that no one beside himself should know what I was doing. He made the arrangements for getting the cash from Loomis and gave me suggestions on how to carry it away discreetly. He was in his sixties and he retired a few months later. I don't really think he had anything to do with my abduction."

"Didn't you once say that a flashback you had while in Loretta Workman's house convinced you that Tom Workman was in the plane?" Chris asked.

I nodded, "Yes. That was when I was still having problems with my memory. Also that's why I remembered the name George."

"Ah," Father interjected, "Can we return to where you said you made three trips from the Seattle bank to Chelan?"

"Well, I feel a little sheepish telling you the truth now. I don't know why I told you that…fib. See, that's what money does to you. That wasn't me. Originally I wanted to take a plane, but I didn't have the guts to do it. I had one hundred thousand less than two million dollars in my thirty-eight pound bag. Instead I rented a car in Seattle and drove home with six million dollars in the trunk of a Honda Accord. Going through those lines at the airport would have been too risky. I could have been stopped, forced to open my bag and then spent the next few hours explaining that money, who I was, and where I lived. They might even call the bank for verification that the money was mine. The Seattle Times could have got involved and then half of the population in Washington State would have known that Brian Douglas had nineteen million dollars, plus a lousy picture of me in the article. I just couldn't do it. Besides I like the drive from Seattle to Chelan. Why did I deceive you? I believe it's all about the money. It does make you think differently."

"Are you telling us," Chris broke in, "that you have six million dollars tucked away in your house?"

"No Chris, I had stupidly speculated that the owner of the 7/11 in Seattle called or sent my name and address to his sister, who we know as Loretta Workman. Maybe Tom Workman got the call or the note from the owner and somehow found out that I had won a jackpot, which was ridiculous. As you now know, Tom was my mailman and as he delivered the mail one day, he found me building an addition to my garage. He was an amateur carpenter and in his curiosity asked me what I was building. I told him I was adding some storage space for the new tools I had recently purchased. We discussed the technicalities of the storage area and he continued his deliveries."

"Was the storage area you were building for your tools?" Chris asked.

"No, in the meantime, I had called the president of the bank where the remainder of my millions were and asked him if I could convert four of the million to smaller bills; Tens, twenties, and fifties. He gave me a date to go to Seattle and I met him on a Monday at five in the morning. I had rented a Ford 150 and it was an easy trip."

"So now you had more bags of money, right?" Father said with a smile.

"That's right, except, now I had to make a new cabinet that faced my car when it was parked in the garage. I'll show it to you the next time you come to the house."

"Wow!" Chris sighed, "so you were going to store the money in your garage?"

"The money dictated everything I was doing, butI'm not done yet. I was doing some very strange things and sometimes I was actually aware of being coerced by the stupid money. As sure as if someone was holding a gun to my head I was doing its bidding."

"Father O'Reilly and I were in your garage and I don't recall seeing anything that looked like it was new," Chris said curiously. Father nodded in agreement.

"That's good. I meant for it to be unnoticeable. I even have outline of each tool on the wall so I can easily it and return that unit to its proper place after use. The cabinet is concealed by all of the tools that cover the storage area and the face is built into the existing wall. It would be hard for someone to detect that there was space behind the tool display."

"So you're saying that you had, or have, six million dollars in that storage area in the garage?"

"Yeah, I had six million dollars hidden in that space, but I think Tom Workman got enough information from his uncle in Seattle to figure out that I had built the storage space and that is why I was abducted, but in the meantime I had converted the cash into Bearer Bonds. Bearer Bonds are negotiable and are like cash in the hands of the person who possesses them, simply stated."

Father O'Reilly and Chris sat quietly, shocked by the whole story.

"If they knew where the money was why did they get you involved. Why did they want you dead? You hadn't seen any of them except for Tom Workman," Chris quizzed.

I agree, except now the money was in a safe I got at Costco. This is what I think happened. I was awakened early in the morning of February 3rd 2012, witnessed four men standing around my bed with hoods over their heads, and eye holes cut out. I was quickly covered with a hood and forced into the front room of my house. One man did all the talking.

"We know you won a multi-million dollar lottery, Mr. Douglas "Where is that money?"

They had secured my hands behind my back and while I was thinking about whether I should go ahead and admit that I did have money, someone lifted my hood up to expose my mouth and told me to open it. Suddenly, I felt the cold barrel of what I was sure was a gun in my mouth."

"We don't want to hurt you Mr. Douglas, but if you have money here, we want you to tell us where it is. Understand?"

I thought, *I still had 13 million in the bank in Seattle. If I told them they would let me go and I would only be out six million and would still be alive.*

"I'm going to untie you from the chair and we're all going to the garage, OK?" They took the hood off and I led them to the garage. I walked to the side of the cabinet and uncovered a lock that kept the tool display front secured. My car had been left in front of the locked garage door over night, so I didn't have to back it out to open the door. I opened the large swinging door.

The man that had been speaking asked me how much was in the suit cases.

"There isn't any money in those suitcases," I responded.

"Are you playing games with us, Mr. Douglas?" he growled.

"No sir, the money is in a safe in the house."

I could hear them whispering and after a few minutes they took me back inside. The man untied me. I led them to the safe and opened it and took out a 8 1/2 by 11 manila envelope and laid it on top of the safe box. The man opened the envelope and looked at the bonds.

"What's the value of these Bearer Bonds?" he asked.

"Six million dollars."

Someone put a cloth over my mouth and nose and when I woke up I was in the plane from which they would subsequently drop me into the Cascade Mountains.

Chris looked at Stewart. "What are Bearer Bonds?"

"Essentially they are cash and the man that did all the talking knew that." "Did they know that there was more in a bank in Seattle?" Father queried.

"I don't know that for sure, but I don't think they cared."

They sat staring at Brian in disbelief.

"Why did you go to the garage if you knew the bonds were in the house?" Chris asked.

"A hunch I had. I thought it might have been the mailman. You know, the odd thing about all that happened to me, all the time spent in rehabilitation, broken bones, the mental anguish? I might have forgiven it all if they had kept their word that they wouldn't harm me. They lied to me. Obviously the amount they took from the safe was enough to appease their greed, but it wasn't enough to make them keep their word. I speculated when Tom Workman had talked to me about the cabinet in the garage, I suspected he had something to do with it. Even so, I think I could have let it all slide and been content with what was left. For months I didn't know what had happened, other than I had fallen out of plane." I looked into my two best friend's anguished eyes', and could see the empathy they held for me. But things had changed when I realized they meant to eliminate me. Now, my whole existence was directed toward finding those responsible and killing the bastards. I was going to enjoy killing them. I knew I couldn't say that to my friends because they would think I'd turned into a sociopath. The idea that these men had robbed me and then lied to me was the last straw. I was not the Brian Douglas of old.

CHAPTER THIRTY

At our last meeting with Detective Marci Harris, she had given me some names of people of interest. Her workload was increasing because of gang activity in town. I would be doing some interviewing of my own. I stared down at the name I had written on my notepad. 'Daphne Dunlap', former employee of George Tilden.

"You Mr. Woods," the woman asked as she opened the front door.

"Yes ma'am."

"I'm Delores Dunlap, Daphne's mother. Daphne will be down in a minute." She ushered me into the spacious living room of a large ranch style home and immediately left the room. I looked around. The house was well furnished with beautiful, expensive furniture and hand picked paintings, some originals, I guessed.

"Sorry to keep you waiting Mr. Woods."

I stood.

"Please sit. Would you like a drink?"

"I'll pass, but thank you."

"Do you mind if I have one?"

"Not at all."

I heard the clinking of glasses. "So you want to know some dirt about George Tilden," she said as she walked back into the front room with a glass of red wine.

"Well, I am gathering information on him."

She sat and sipped her drink. "I don't have a lot of good things to say about George. He's a rat, and I'm being kind."

I took note of this woman. She was very attractive and reminded me of a Hollywood starlet. She was at least five six and perfectly figured with beautiful blonde hair.

"I know a lot about George Tilden, most of it bad. Sure he's a philanthropist at certain times of the year, but it's all about business and he is a very good businessman. Everything he does, he does to promote himself, and make more money. I know everyone in business does that, but he's different. He'll do it at any cost. I slept with the bastard for two years and got to know the real George Tilden. I hope I'm not shocking you Mr. Woods"

Well, she was shocking me. I wondered if this was her first glass of wine or if she had been drinking before I arrived.

"I'm not drunk, Mr. Woods. This is who I am. Mr. Tilden brings the worst out in me. He can't sue me for what I say because I know so much about him that could hurt his business, and his personal life if it got out. I didn't need the job as his secretary. I just wanted out of the house. My mother and I own seventy-three acres of pears, apples and cherries, plus the large Dunlap warehouse you saw on the way here. That keeps us well heeled, Mr. Woods. My father, rest his soul, died a few years ago and left us all this. He loved being a rancher and orchardist and did very well for himself. My mother runs our orchards every bit as well as my father did. I love my mother, and despite my being spoiled and unruly, she loves me. I guess that's what mother's do…love."

She stopped talking and just stared at me. I thought she might cry.

"No, I'm not going to cry Mr. Woods. I stopped feeling sorry for myself a long time ago."

For sure, Daphne Dunlap was keenly aware of my stare. I didn't know whether to ask her questions or if she was waiting to say something else. As I pondered a very pretty young woman walked into the room.

"I'm sorry Mother, I didn't know you had company."

"This is Stewart Woods, Natalie. My daughter, Natalie Hudson."

I stood as she came toward me and offered her hand. "Nice to meet Mr. Woods." She turned to her mother. "Grams, Aunt Helen and I are going to Macy's in East Wenatchee. Would you like us to call you later to meet for an early dinner?"

"That would be fine, honey."

"Sorry for the interruption Mr. Woods," Natalie offered, and she strolled out of room.

"You have a lovely daughter, Ms. Dunlap."

"She takes after her father and my mother. I'm divorced and have taken my father's name back. Natalie loved her father and kept his name. He was one of the first to die in the Gulf War."

"I'm sorry," I said solemnly.

"I know enough about George Tilden and Bart Colangelo to send those two to Walla Walla for years," Daphne stated out of the blue.

I was jolted by the impact of her statement, and gazed at her, the shock clear on my face.

"You heard me right, Mr. Woods. But if I told you I would be jeopardizing my life. You see, Tilden or Colangelo are each capable of killing me with no hesitation. Most people think he's some generous philanthropist, and in some ways he does work at putting forth that image. But make no mistake, the man is ruthless and if he thought he could get away with it, he'd dump me out of his plane, or weigh me down with a block of concrete, and toss me into the Columbia River."

I wrote down what she said on my notepad.

"What are you writing Mr. Woods?" Are you a detective or what?" she demanded.

I knew that I would be the only person with this information and that I wouldn't divulge it to anyone that could get Ms. Dunlap in trouble. I still had my badge from working for ATF and I had brought it with me just in case she asked this question.

"I work for ATF and I'm investigating the disappearance of one of our agents."

She stood and walked over to where I was sitting on the love seat and sat. She looked at the badge and then looked at me. I felt she was thinking I was lying.

"Is this a government agency?" she asked.

I looked into her beautiful green eyes and answered. "Yes."

Daphne was more beautiful up close and was fully aware of what she did to men up close.

"I'll tell you more if you have a drink with me Mr. Woods."

She stood and looked down at me for a few seconds. "Scotch or Whiskey?"

I was more a beer and wine man but I decided I wanted to hear what she had to say about Tilden and Colangelo.

"Whiskey will be fine."

The phone rang while she was in the kitchen. I could hear her voice, but was unable make out what she was saying. Then there was silence for a few minutes. I stood and walked to the fireplace and scanned the framed pictures of the family.

"Those were better times Mr. Woods. We were a family and everyone got along," Daphne said as she walked into the front room wearing a very bright red silk robe. "But like life, it can all change in an instant." She handed me the whiskey and we stood looking at each other. She could have been Marilyn Monroe. She was stunning and very sure of herself. Her blonde hair was wavy and hung over her right eye and her full red, lips were slightly open. I think I was holding my breath because I suddenly felt dizzy. She approached and led me to the love seat.

"Are you all right, Mr. Woods?"

"I'm fine." I sat and took a good pull on the drink. It must have been straight whiskey except for the two cubes of floating ice. I coughed.

"You're not a whiskey drinker are you, Mr. Woods"

I smiled. "Your very perceptive, Ms. Dunlap."

"I've been called intuitive, and please call me Daphne."

"Then it's only fair that you call me Stew or Stewart."

"Mother called to tell me that she and my daughter are in Chelan and are going to be staying in our cabin on the Lake and won't be home tonight. They're going water skiing tomorrow with a friend of my daughter's that they ran into at Macys. Would you like to spend the night with me Stew," she said with a sexy smile on her face.

I was speechless. She stood and took off her red robe, held her out her hand. All I could do was stare at the most beautiful body I had ever seen.

"Why Stewart I believe you're drooling," she laughed shamelessly as she led me into a large bedroom.

CHAPTER THIRTY-ONE

"I was beginning to think you weren't coming back Bart," Tilden whined.

"What the hell's that suppose to mean. I told you how long I was going to be gone."

"Yeah, but you didn't tell me you were taking Loretta Workman with you."

"What…you're my father now? I gotta tell you who I'm dating. You sound like the damned government. You have to know everything I'm doing? Well, wake yourself up, I don't have to tell you shit. OK? I've been back for two weeks and doing a lot of snooping around. Guess who went to see Daphne Dunlap the other day?"

"I don't know who you're talking about."

"Do you know who Stewart Woods is?"

"Tell me all you know about Stewart Woods."

"Let's get out of here office and go where we can talk freely. How about the loop? We can find a bench or walk if you like."

They sat at one of the trail benches. The sun was out but not excessively hot yet.

"Like I said, I've been busy poking around. Loretta has filled me in on whose in the hunt for Brian Douglas. So far, no one knows what happened to him. I don't even think anyone knows he had won a multi-million dollar lottery. This is what I do know. The priest, Father Damon O'Reilly, who you've met, is friend to Christina Palmer and Stewart Woods and those three are in collaboration with Detective Marci Harris of the Chelan Police Department. One of Loretta's neighbors thinks Woods is related to Ms. Palmer, maybe cousin or even brother."

Tilden nodded, "What about this Woods character?"

"Getting back to Daphne Dunlap. Why do you think this Stewart fellow would want to talk to your ex-secretary? Is there any way she could get you in trouble? Does she have anything on you?"

Tilden was thinking about his ex-secretary and wondering the same thing. He knew that she could easily make waves for him and Colangelo. On one of his drunken nights with Daphne he had blabbed about how Bart and two others had made a man disappear in the Cascade Mountains.

Bart was watching Tilden closely as the wheels were turning in the man's head. What was he going to tell me that he was thinking so hard about?

"Why did you ever let her go? She was Hollywood beautiful and very smart. I never did hear why she stopped working for you."

Tilden smiled and twirled his thumbs on the table. "Well it's a long story. I would have married her at the drop of a hat, but my wife put a stop to all that. One of my shortcomings is that I like beautiful woman and they've always liked me. It's a curse. Most men find a woman and fall in love. They stay married for years and years. Diane, my wife was the Washington State Queen in the Miss America contest a few years ago. She's still a beautiful woman and in my own way I love her. But beautiful women have always lured me into their bedrooms quite easily. If Daphne Dunlap put her eyes on you and wanted you, well, you were just a willing partner."

"What do you mean your wife put an end to it? How?"

"Beautiful women are also very smart in many ways. They learn how to use the God given beauty to their best advantage. As they grow up, they are cute, then pretty, very attractive and finally beautiful; men drool, women take a second look. They learn to smile a lot because they're looked at a lot. Most men are intimidated by really beautiful women and won't approach them, but for most, the opposite is true. They are very friendly for the reasons I just mentioned and most are polite. The smarter they are the easier they are to approach. In answer to your question, Daphne had worked for me off and on for over three years. She and her mother own a large diversified fruit orchard in Cashmere and she would have to quit at certain times of the year to help harvest their crops. Well, Diane had never seen Daphne in person and one day she waltzed into my office, took one look at her, and promptly had me fire her."

Bart eyed Tilden curiously. "Just like that, you fired her?"

"Well, it took a few day, because I was reluctant to let Daphne go. Certainly you can understand that."

"Yeah, I suppose so, she is drop dead beautiful," he smiled. "What did Daphne say to convince you?"

It was Tilden's turn to consider what he should say to a man who might want to use whatever he said against him. "Let's just say she had the goods on me, so I let Daphne go. By the way, I have met this Woods person. He has been to my house. Came to talk to Diane about a person with a Canyon Road address he was looking for. She introduced us as he was leaving. That's all I know about Stewart Woods. Tell me what you know about him."

"Like I said earlier, I followed him around for two days. That's how I knew he'd been to see Dunlap. Loretta Workman thinks he's the man that came to see her but she didn't get his name. She said he was tall and very good-looking. Does that sound like it could be him?"

"Well you followed him around. Do you think he's good-looking?"

"I haven't seen him up close. You met him and shook his hand. Is he good-looking?"

Tilden smiled, "well, he's not really my type, but I guess you could say he's handsome, at least Diane thinks he is."

"Did you think he was someone we should worry about?"

Tilden directed his eyes toward the open landscape outside and considered the question. "I think I know where this is going, Bart. We need to find out where Woods came from and if he's on to us."

CHAPTER THIRTY-TWO

"Thanks for coming in Mr. Woods," Detective Don Jones said as he closed the door behind him. "Sit down, please." He walked around his desk and sat.

"How long have you known Daphne Dunlap, Mr. Woods?"

"I met her for the first time a little over a week ago. Let's see, it was on a Sunday and today is Wednesday. Ten days ago."

"Do you always remember exactly how long ago you meet someone?"

"No sir I don't, but Daphne Dunlap is someone who leaves a lasting impression." I smiled with the sweet memory.

Jones noticed the smile. "It was a good meeting I gather."

"It was. Is there a problem with Ms. Dunlap?"

"Have you seen her since then?"

I moved forward in my chair, "No I haven't."

"What was the purpose of your meeting?"

"I discovered that we had a mutual friend and wanted to find out what she knew about him."

"Can I ask you who that person was?" Jones asked.

I looked at the detective and paused, "George Tilden."

He nodded, "Delores Dunlap, Daphne's mother reported her missing a few days after her meeting with you."

"Missing?" I said incredulously. I looked directly at the detective and saw that he was observing me closely. "I had nothing to do with her disappearance. Did you ever meet her, Detective? She's beautiful." If she was missing I had a hunch I knew who was responsible. It renewed my commitment for vengeance. I couldn't believe the bastard would ... "Would it be all right with you if I talked to Delores Dunlap, Detective?"

"Absolutely. You can talk to whom ever you want. You're not planning on leaving any time soon, are you?"

"No sir, I'm not." I stood.

"I wonder if I could confirm your address before you leave, Mr. Woods." He read the address correctly then asked for my land and cell telephone numbers.

I sat in my car and thought about Daphne. Something was really wrong. I still had her telephone number in my notepad. I dialed it and a woman answered.

"Mrs. Dunlap?"

"Yes."

"This is Stewart Woods. Do you remember me?"

She didn't respond for a few seconds. "Has Detective Jones talked to you, Mr. Woods?"

"I just left his office and I was wondering if I could come and talk to you?"

"I, don't know," she stammered.

"Mrs. Dunlap, I assure you I had nothing to do with your daughter's disappearance, but I think I know who does. If today is not the right time, I can come whenever it's convenient for you, or perhaps you can suggest somewhere more public if that would be more comfortable for you."

"You did say you talked to Detective Jones, didn't you?"

"Yes ma'am, and I asked permission to talk to you. He is aware that I want to see you."

"I suppose there is no harm in talking to you, Mr. Woods."

"I could be there in twenty minutes."

"That will be fine."

Mrs. Dunlap led me into the front room where another woman was sitting. She favored Mrs. Dunlap. There was also a large man in coveralls standing by the entry to their kitchen, holding a wide brimmed working hat in his hands.

"Thank you for seeing me, Mrs. Dunlap."

"This is my sister, Helen Piccotti, Mr. Woods. I hope you don't mind her sitting in. She knows just about all that I know." Helen Piccotti stood and offered her hand, but said nothing and promptly sat back down. Mrs. Dunlap motioned the large man over to us. This is my foreman, Lorenzo Gonzalvez, Mr.

Woods." He shook my hand and peered at me. Mrs. Dunlap thanked him and he left the room.

"Do you think you might know who took my daughter?"

"Yes ma'am, but I'm not one hundred percent sure."

She stood. "Would you like a drink of some kind, or coffee Mr. Woods?"

"Coffee would be fine."

The two women walked off to the kitchen. I stood and made my way to the fireplace mantel and looked at a large picture of Daphne. It took me back to the night I had spent with her here.

"She is a beautiful woman Mr. Woods," she said quietly as she entered the room with two cups of coffee.

"People have often told me she is reminiscent of Marilyn Monroe."

"Yes ma'am."

We sat. "The problem with beauty is that it attracts all kinds of people. Daphne has met some very fine men in her life, but also some very bad ones. I liked her husband but he was killed in one those dreadful wars this country is always fighting. I've never quite understood these men that go to war. Frank Hudson was a fine man, handsome, generous, loving, and yet he kept going back to those awful wars. I often thought he had a death wish." She took a sip of her coffee.

"Did she date a lot of men?"

"No, no she didn't. She liked you Mr. Woods."

Our eyes met. "I'm flattered Mrs. Dunlap. Your daughter could have dated any man she wanted."

Mrs. Dunlap smiled at me. "She said you were a sweet, innocent man."

I was never comfortable with compliments or flattery.

"I'm sorry Mr. Woods, I've embarrassed you. So who do you think has taken Daphne?"

Our eyes locked. I had no qualms about telling her but I was afraid it might come back to bite me. I could get her in more trouble than she could handle, by telling her about Tilden.

"If your reluctance teeters on my safety, I can understand

that, but I assure you, I'm able to take care of myself, Mr. Woods. If you were thinking it might be George Tilden, then spit it out. I happen to agree with that thinking. If it's not Tilden, then I would like to know who you think it might be."

"I can see how your daughter comes by her intuition, Mrs. Dunlap."

"You're speaking in the present tense, Mr. Woods. I happen to believe she is dead. Daphne and I were very close. You don't have to spare my feelings. I did all my crying a few days ago. I lost my husband to cancer five years ago, my parents three years ago in a car accident, and Daphne's husband to a war. Yes, each death is painful, but that doesn't stop this big ball from spinning around the sun. Life goes on."

I was stunned by the overt expression of her private feelings. Her cell phone rang. She reached into her purse and looked to see who was calling. "Excuse me, Mr. Woods. It's my orchard foreman." She stood and walked into the kitchen. "Oh my God!" she said clearly from the kitchen and then returned the front room. "I'm sorry Mr. Woods but you'll have to excuse me," she sobbed quietly."

"Is there anything I can do?"

"You'll have to leave immediately. I'm sorry."

I walked to the front door alone and as I opened the door to leave, I turned around; but she had already disappeared from the room.

CHAPTER THIRTY-THREE

Vandy Earhart, Bart Colangelo and George Tilden were sitting on a bench/table on the East Wenatchee side, near the sight of the old bridge.

"I know there something's going on and I want to know what you two are doing?" Vandy exclaimed through gritted teeth.

Tilden looked over at Bart.

"I don't know what you're talking about Vandy."

"I'm not stupid, Bart. I read the papers."

"So what are you specifically referring to?" Tilden asked.

"I didn't want to think anything when I read that Caldwell Richardson had drowned. But when I read that Dunlap woman had gone missing, and still hasn't been located, I thought about you George. I remember when she worked for you. She was a damned pretty woman and the scuttlebutt was that you and she had words. That it wasn't a happy separation."

Bart eyed Vandy. "So you think because George fired this girl he might have something to do with her disappearance."

"That's right Bart. I also happen to know that you knew who Cal Richardson was. I can't prove that you had anything to do with his drowning. *Maybe* it *was* an accident."

"But you think since I knew who he was, that I might have pushed him overboard without a life vest."

Tilden spoke up, "Let's say you're right, that I snuffed Daphne Dunlap and Bart here, drowned Richardson. Are you saying that somehow you're in the clear about all this?"

"No I'm not saying that. I've seen enough movies and TV crime shows to know I'm connected to you two. I'd just like to know why I'm not told about these things."

"I think I know why you're complaining. You're worried that you might be next. Is that it?" Tilden asked calmly.

"It did cross my mind. One mishap I can understand, but

two is worrisome. When does it stop? Whose next?"

"Well, Vandy to clear up your bad thoughts about George and I, we didn't snuff out anybody. We don't know what happened to that funny man that barked and swore. George didn't drop Dunlap from his plane over the Cascade Mountains, and we're not going to get rid of you. We're all too tightly tied together. If you were suddenly killed, the authorities would surely come to us for information, because we're friends. Does that make sense Vandy?"

Vandy nodded, "When you put it that way, I guess it does."

"You think too much and it causes you to worry. Stop worrying about things you don't have any control over. Go home and have a shot of JD and stop all the thinking." George stood, walked around the table and patted Vandy on the shoulder as he stood.

Vandy nodded, "you're right, I worry too much. I feel better now that I've talked to you and Bart."

George and Bart watched Vandy walk across the lawn to his car.

"The good thing is that Vandy can't do anything about what is bothering him. You and I are the only people he can talk to about it," George smiled.

"How well do you know Vandy, George?"

"I know he owns a tire business and that he does a thriving business. He told me he bought it from his uncle a few years ago."

"Did you know that he did a stretch in Walla Walla?"

"Really?"

Bart looked George in the eyes. "Robbed a bank, killed a guard and spent eight years behind bars."

"Well live and learn," George smiled, "and where are you going with this?"

"Maybe we should be worried about our distressed friend. He's killed once and may not be afraid to do it again."

"Naw, Bart. I don't think so. Shooting some guard is one thing, but he isn't smart enough to pull off killing us."

"Think about it George; he kills us and dumps our bodies in the Columbia and a hundred miles down stream the fishes eat our flesh and all that's left is bones at the bottom of the river."

"I'm telling you Bart, he's not the type to do that. He doesn't have the stuff---or the motive to do that."

"Motive? Him or us, that's motivation, and you heard him say it did cross his mind that we might want to get rid of him. He's got motivation."

Suddenly Vandy was back. He parked his car and came trotting toward us. "I've been so damned busy lately that I forgot to tell you about a note I found on my windshield." He placed the note on the table. George picked it up and handed it to Bart. Bart read it out loud, "I know what you've done." It was written with a marking pencil.

"How long have you had this," George asked.

"I don't remember exactly. Maybe two weeks, maybe longer, Vandy replied.

"Where were you when you found it?"

Vandy shook his head. "South end Safeway."

Bart chimed in, "Look this note could have been for someone else's car or it could be from a girlfriend or someone playing a game with you. Don't go getting sweaty about some stupid note, Vandy."

"Yeah I suppose so…but what if it isn't?"

"We didn't get any notes, Vandy," Bart argued.

Vandy eyed them dubiously. "Neither of you got any notes?"

"Right, neither of us got a note," George agreed.

"Shit! I've got to get hold of myself. Vandy turned and strode to his car.

Tilden stood, "What do you think?"

"Why would Vandy get a note and we didn't. I believe exactly what I said to him. There's a lot of Ford Mustangs like his, plus no one has contacted him since. It was a mistake or a prank, and we should forget about it."

"I hope you're right."

CHAPTER THIRTY-FOUR

"Thank you for meeting me here at Washington Park, Mr. Tilden. I want you to know that Detective Don Jones of the police department is aware of my meeting here with you."

"I don't understand Mrs. Dunlap.'"

"I guess it does sound a little presumptuous of me, but I think you are some how involved with the disappearance of my daughter."

They walked to a table and sat, one on each side facing each other.

"I don't know why you would think that Mrs. Dunlap. I loved your daughter. I wouldn't hurt her for anything."

"You're a strange man Mr. Tilden. You're married and yet you can say you loved my daughter without any hesitation. To me that seems odd."

"I didn't mean to fall in love with her but I would have given up my marriage for your daughter's hand. As it turned out, I was unable to work out an equitable settlement with my wife. She wanted everything I had, and it would have been like starting all over again."

"You're confirming what I think about you Mr. Tilden. I know my daughter was beautiful and like a lot of men like you, they want to own them. Surely you have met other attractive ladies. Did you want to throw away your marriage for them? My husband was very handsome but he didn't want to discard me for some other woman every time he met one. Don't you have any discipline? Where is your integrity, your loyalty?"

"Mrs. Dunlap did you call me here to scold me about my character or do you have some legitimate question?" George Tilden stood and waited for her answer.

"You're right Mr. Tilden. I won't mince words with you. Did you murder my Daphne?"

Her words might as well have been a punch in the face, but he remained cool. "No ma'am, I did not murder your daughter. According to the Wenatchee World and the police department, she is only missing."

"Daphne told me about you Mr. Tilden and I have every reason to believe you murdered her. I don't know how you did it, but I'm looking into it now. If and when I have enough information I will see to it that you never kill anyone else. It seems you have others who are trying to find out things about you. I'm hoping this will work on your conscience, if you even have one. Just in case you think you can do away with me, Mr. Tilden, I have written a statement to the affect that you would be responsible. Both Detectives Donald Jones of the Wenatchee Police Department and Marci Harris have been apprised, as well as my sister and my orchard foreman, Lorenzo Gonzalvez."

Goerge stood abruptly and peered at Mrs. Dunlap. "I only hope that I am as far away from you as I can be if something bad does happen to you and I can assure you Mrs. Dunlap I would never hurt you. I'm sorry you feel the way you do. Now if you don't have anything else to say, I'll be on my way."

Mrs. Dunlap sat at the table for a few minutes, then walked drearily to the foreman waiting by her car.

"Thank you for bringing me here, Lorenzo. I'm sorry I kept you this long," she lamented.

Lorenzo opened the back door for Mrs. Dunlap, "So this is the bad man you talked about."

"Yes, and after the tongue-lashing I gave him he…" she sighed, closed her eyes and laid her head against the cushioned back seat.

Lorenzo closed his door and looked into the rearview mirror observing her sadness, holding his gaze for a few seconds, then turned the key and the engine sprang to life.

CHAPTER THIRTY-FIVE

Lorenzo Gonzalvez sat in his car observing the Tilden building, not too far from Wal-mart and a sports center. His Bushnell binoculars lay on the front seat and a thermos of black coffee was cradled against the front passenger seat. He had been at this task for just over two weeks and knew to a certain degree, what Mr. Tilden's daily routine entailed. Stocking was part of his previous training.

He opened the thermos, took a swallow of the black drink and his thoughts went back in time to when he was a Seal in Iraq. He remembered Navy boot camp in San Diego and requesting to become a Seal. The training to become a member of this elite force was nothing short of brutal. More men wash out than make it to the end, but those that do are special and he had felt that pride. He still felt the camaraderie within the Seal's company. He had become a sniper, brought his .300 Win Mag when he left the Navy, and had only on rare occasions fired it, but never on the local rifle range. The first time he had killed was the hardest. All the subsequent kills had been good. Good in the sense that he was stopping a killer from killing Americans.

As he observed Tilden getting into his car, he was drawn back to the present.

CHAPTER THIRTY-SIX

"Stewart, can you meet me at Central Washington Hospital on Miller Street in Wenatchee?" "It's about Father O'Reilly."

"Chris, what's the problem?"

"I'm not really sure. His heart I think," she sobbed.

"I'll be there as fast as I can."

I was trying to think of Father O'Reilly's age. He had to be at least seventy and he had mentioned that he took some kind of heart pill. I was feeling bad about not seeing him lately but my own situation had me forgetting everything but getting revenge. It was eating me alive and I couldn't shake it. How long had it been since I had seen Chris or Father? I hadn't been to church since I don't know when.

I walked through the revolving front door and looked around for Chris. When she saw me she stood and I hurried over to her. Her eyes were red from crying and her hair was disheveled.

"We're not able to see him right now Stewart, but I thought we might find a visiting room and wait till we can."

"Sure, that's fine."

"The doctor told me he might not make it," Chris said as they sat down.

"It's that serious?"

"Where have you been Stewart? Do you know that it is weeks since we've seen you? No, Over two months. I thought you were going to keep us in the loop."

Two months, I thought. *Had it been that long? I felt like hell. My two closest friends and I hadn't even been aware I was avoiding them. Crap. I couldn't even look at her.*

"I knew there was something going on with him because I could see that his skin color had changed in the last week when I saw him at mass. He wasn't eating and looked like he was losing weight. I mentioned it to him but he just brushed it off with old age.

"I guess you didn't get any of the messages I left on your phone."

The truth is I do remember some of the notes but I was so charged I let them slide. I didn't make time to return the calls. I was such a bastard.

"Brian I think you've changed. I'm not blaming you for that, but you're different now. When I give it thought, it's perfectly understandable. I believe anyone would change after all you've been through, and you're still ensconced in this vendetta or whatever it is."

I was so embarrassed by her statement. Was I becoming someone else without realizing it? I sat forward in my cushioned chair looking down at the carpet, elbows on my knees. I wanted to say something to Chris, but the words wouldn't come. She stopped talking. We sat there in silence. I was suffocating with shame and disgrace. I knew she was having a tough time telling me this.

The door opened and a man in white coat with a stethoscope wrapped around his neck walked in and came directly to us. We stood.

"Ms. Palmer we've done everything we can do for Father O'Reilly, and now we have to wait until he either pulls out or succumbs to a very bad Myocardial Infarction. He's sleeping now. I'm going to be very blunt with you, Ms. Palmer. He's almost eighty years old and I don't give him much hope. Go home and the nurse will call you if he comes out of it. There is no need for you to stay here." The doctor turned and left.

I stood wanting very much to cry, but didn't. The doctor, by not talking to me, made me feel even smaller than I had before. Chris pulled a tissue from her purse, dabbed her eyes and blew her nose.

"I think I'm going to take the doctor's advice and go home, Brian. I have classes tomorrow and I haven't been sleeping well. I'm glad you were able to come tonight. Father

O'Reilly would have appreciated seeing you." She gave me a quick kiss on the cheek and hurried away.

I sat down and thought of the words the doctor had said. My friend may never wake up. I stood, walked to the nurse's station and asked directions to Father O'Reilly's room.

He was thinner than the last time I had seen him over two months ago. His face was pale and his breathing was shallow and even. I pulled the metal chair close to the bed and sat.

Father O'Reilly had known my parents all their lives, and had shared with me his wish to become a priest when he was fourteen years old. He was the quintessential priest: kind, thoughtful, caring, and God loving. He loved his parish in a quiet kind of way, enough that all knew he cared. He did love a cold Budweiser or glass of Merlot, but not in excess, and he loved to eat. He loved sports, especially fishing and kept in good shape with long walks and hiking.

"Would you like a cup of coffee, sir?" a nurse asked in a hushed voice.

I looked up at the compassionate face and stared into her brown eyes for a few seconds, "No thank you, I was just about to leave, but thank you." I looked at the nametag on her uniform, Lori Harris. "You wouldn't be related to the detective in the town of Chel- "

"She's my sister," she interjected. "Why would you think Marci and I are related?"

I stood, "you favor her, I suppose, or maybe you both have the same coloring." I responded still wondering why I had asked the question. "I hope I didn't offend you."

She shook her head, "Are you a friend of Marci's?"

"Yes."

A light began flashing on the wall.

"Ooops that light's for me. It was nice talking to you sir," she said and disappeared as quickly as she had arrived.

It was a week later and I was at the Wenatchee Cemetery on Western Avenue. Father O'Reilly had died. I was standing near the burial site, beside a large Redwood tree. I was so ashamed of myself for not having visited the good priest at the end of his life. There had to be at least five hundred people surrounding the grave as the eulogies were recited.

Then a lone bugle blew the first three notes and a clear soprano voice began singing Taps. Day is done…gone the sun…from the lakes…from the hills…from the sky…all is well…safely rest…God is nigh. As the second verse started I headed to my car. I was finally crying for my odious behavior of these last few weeks.

It is almost three years later and Brian Douglas's abduction has not been avenged. Five people are dead: Father O'Reilly, possibly from stress, Delores, from grief and Daphne Dunlap, a question mark, and Daphne's daughter, Natalie Hudson, tried to hang herself in her grandmother's orchard from grief. Even Cal Richardson's drowning, might be related.

Tilden, Colangelo and Earhart are responsible.

"Those three must die," I shouted as I lay down my composed obituaries. I was focused now and I knew what I had to do.

I returned to my rental in Wenatchee and went over all the notes I had accrued on my three suspects. Everything I had in front of me was confirmation that these three, Tilden, Colangelo and Earhart had abducted me to kill me. I was stalling and didn't know why. I was confused and angry as I stared out my front window to the town below. My stomach growled. Glancing at my watch, I knew why.

I was driving to the Windmill to get a steak. As I crossed the north end bridge, I noticed a silver Nissan behind. I was almost sure that the driver of the car was aware I knew he was following me. I reached my destination and parked. A tall man in coveralls stepped out of the Nissan and approached me. As he drew near I recognized his face from the Dunlap residence in Cashmere, but his name escaped me.

Extending his hand, "Mr. Woods, I hope you remember me, sir."

"I do but I don't remember your name."

"It was a brief encounter and I wouldn't expect that you would. Lorenzo Gonzalvez," he replied. "Would you mind if I joined you for dinner? I'm starving."

"I could use the company," I responded happily.

Minutes later in the restaurant they each took a sip of the red wine that Lorenzo had recommended.

"It's a Portuguese wine that is well liked in my country, Mr. Woods."

I nodded, "It's good."

"Thank you for allowing me to eat with you. I've been tracking you for a few days and today I made up my mind to talk to you. I believe we're after the same thing. Justice."

"You're taller than I remember, Mr. Gonzalvez."

"I'm six three and about two twenty."

"What have you determined about me besides I want justice?"

"Not a lot, I did talk to Detective Jones at the police department. Didn't learn a lot. I know you've had George Tilden and Bart Colangelo under surveillance and you put a note on Vanderbilt Earhart's windshield."

That caught my attention.

"You're good Mr. Gonzalvez, very good."

Our steaks arrived and I as I ate, he devoured a twelve ounce steak in just a few bites, drank the remainder of the wine and then we ordered Peach pie and coffee.

"Mr. Woods I like you. I did try to find out who you were but after Detective Jones at the police department couldn't fill me in, I really didn't care who you were. I knew you had my feelings at heart. I knew I could trust you. Trust is a big part of my life Mr. Woods. It's what I liked about the Dunlap family; total faith in their word. I mean to avenge their deaths."

Gonzalvez sipped his coffee and watched me to see if I was buying all that he was selling.

"I was a Navy Seal in a couple of recent wars and became a sniper. I enjoyed killing bad people, and because I did my job well, I was decorated and respected. All of the accolades

I received were great and made me proud, but they were fleeting honors. You don't live by hand shakes and medals, Mr. Woods."

This man had integrity and it oozed out of him. I liked him.

"What do you live by, Mr. Gonzalvez?"

"I have no family of my own, but the Dunlap family filled that void. I was content working at their fruit ranch. I had purpose to my life and I enjoyed their hospitality. I felt very much like I was one of them and now that feeling has been shattered. I have spent the last twenty nine days following three people: Tilden, Colangelo and a young man by the name of Earhart, and of course I was also following you, Mr. Woods."

"Would you gentlemen like anything else?" the waitress asked.

I looked at Gonzalvez and he shook his head.

"No thank you. Bring me the bill Miss."

Outside the restaurant Gonzalvez followed me to my car.

"Thank you for listening to me Mr. Woods and thank you for the dinner. I just have one question for you sir."

I looked into his eyes as they studied me.

"Are we done talking about the three men I just mentioned?"

I was pretty sure I knew what he meant but I didn't really have an answer.

"Whether you go in with me or not Mr. Woods I'm giving them until the seventeenth of September," and he hurried away.

I stood by my car and then hurried to his Nissan. "Can I have your telephone number or where I can reach you Mr. Gonzalvez?'

"I have the number at your house, but I'd like your cell number, Sir." He retrieved a small notepad and waited for me to give him the numbers.

"Thanks Mr. Woods, I'll call you in a couple of days."

As he drove out of the parking lot, I was still thinking about all that he had said. I took out my notepad and wrote down the seventeenth of September. He didn't say what he was going to do, but I knew what he meant.

I lay in bed thinking about what Lorenzo Gonzalvez had suggested and I was having trouble with the whole thing. He admitted he trusted me. With or without me he was going to do what I had been planning all along, but didn't have the guts to do. The man had no hesitation about what he wanted to do. Why was I feeling like such a coward? He knew I wouldn't say anything because he knew that I wanted to do the same thing: I really did but…

I turned on the light, went to the kitchen and poured a half glass of whiskey. I sipped and as it traveled down my throat it took my breath away: I coughed. I was in need of some conversation about my recent ordeal: but who? Who in the hell could I talk to that would go along with any of this madness? Christina came to mind but I had done a good job of estranging her and Father O'Reilly. Dr. Lansing came to mind. Could I talk to her and get some recommendations? Naw, she wouldn't listen to this crazy idea. Could it be that I would have to do this on my own? Yes. I alone would have to determine what I was going to do about Tilden, Colangelo and Earhart. I knew I could let Lorenzo Gonzalvez do it and be completely free of it all. He was only too ready to do it without me. Yet, this was my nightmare. I couldn't be free of it until I put my mark on it.

I called Detective Don Jones and made an appointment to see him.

"I wish I could tell you that I have something more than the last time we talked Mr. Woods. I can't believe it has been three plus years since he disappeared. I have some information that points to George J. Tilden, but not enough to bring him in. It's been over a year since I've entered anything on his file, and that was when Mrs. Delores Dunlap alerted me to her conference with Mr. Tilden at the Washington Park."

I left his office disappointed at least I knew there was nothing new. I was desperate to do something, but what. My cell phone rang. It was Lorenzo Gonzalvez. I hadn't called him back in the two days.

"Yes, Mr. Gonzalvez."

"Could you meet me at the Igloo on Wenatchee Avenue in fifteen minutes Mr. Woods?"

I knew what he wanted and I was still spineless. Lately making any kind of decisions was getting to be impossible. It wasn't me.

"Fifteen minutes?"

"Yes, do you need more time?"

"No. I'll be there Mr. Gonzalvez."

When I arrived, he was sitting in a booth in the back of the tavern, nursing a tap beer. He held his hand up to me. There were only two other customers a man and a woman at the bar. It was still morning.

I sat opposite him.

"Thanks for coming, Mr. Woods. I won't keep you long."

"Just coffee please," I requested from the bar maid when she arrived. He hadn't drunk any of his beer. I put both of my elbows on the table with my arms flat and looked at him as he thought about what he was going to say. The waitress placed the black coffee on the table and left.

"I'm not good with words Mr. Woods, but I have good instincts. As I told you, I was a sniper during two wars and I judge quickly and usually make good decisions. Killing has been a big part of my life. It came easy to me from the very start. Bad people should be killed but we're too civilized to do it except at wartime. Good people don't kill other good people. I think I'm good people, and I felt that the Dunlap's were good people. In our culture we can't kill bad people even if we're sure the person killed someone. With no witness they go free. I realize that you are not suited for killing like me Mr. Woods, and so I'm giving you a pass on joining me. You're intentions are good though and I respect you for that. I have only one request sir."

Our eyes locked, froze for a few seconds. "I understand completely Mr. Gonzalvez."

He stood and I followed suit. We shook hands and he walked out the door. I sat down and took a sip of the coffee. Of course I would never say anything. *Where was Father O'Reilly when I needed him?* I thought. I longed for someone to discuss what was happening, I needed a sounding board.

CHAPTER THIRTY-SEVEN

I woke up and looked at the red digital numbers on the clock at my bedside. It was 2:47 AM. I listened. Had I heard something, or was I dreaming. I stood and walked out of my bedroom and entered the front room, walked through to the kitchen in the dark.

"Don't turn around, Mr. Woods," a voice warned.

I felt something prodding my back. *Probably a gun,* I thought.

"I want you to put this hood over your head," he said as he placed a hood in my right hand.

The voice had a distinguishable southern twang. I slipped the hood over my head.

"I'm going to move you over to your kitchen table, Mr. Woods. Please sit down."

"Are you here to rob me?" I asked.

"Sir, I'll do all the asking for now…though I will tell you I've been following you around for a while; in answer to your question. No, I'm not here to rob you. I would like to ask you some questions and I would like you to answer them honestly. Do we understand each other, Mr. Woods?"

"I guess it will depend on the questions," I said unnerved.

"That wasn't my finger I poked you with Mr. Woods. Please be aware of that. I'm not supposed to lay a hand on you. My employer doesn't want your pretty face to show any marks and being the good subordinate that I am, I won't touch any part of you, sir. It is my understanding that you have a relative by the name of Christina Palmer who lives in Chelan. She's a fine looking woman, and I know you wouldn't want anything bad to happen to her. Right?"

"I'll do my best to answer your questions." I replied.

"It seems that no one knows anything about you and that's why I'm here. You just came out of nowhere, took flying lessons. How come you wanted to learn to fly?"

"I always wanted to fly. I'm from Seattle and Wenatchee has this small airport with very little traffic and that was the reason I wanted to learn."

"That seems reasonable, Mr. Woods."

I heard him as he stood and walked over to the light switch. Though I couldn't see a thing, I could tell the light in the kitchen was on. He returned and I could hear the sound of paper unfolding and something metal being placed on the kitchen table. I was trying to think what it could be.

"What's you interest in finding out what happened to Brian Douglas?" he asked.

"Christina was dating the man before he disappeared. I was assisting her in finding out anything about him."

"That's good Mr. Woods. How long has she known this Douglas fella?"

"I'm not sure, I think she had once mentioned about four months."

"Good, you're doing fine sir. Have you had any success?"

"Not really."

"Have you ever considered that this Brian feller might be dead?"

"Yes, we did consider that possibility."

"I understand you've talked to some individuals, that you and this Miss Palmer thought might be involved?"

I was thinking about the question. Had Christina or I ever talked to any of the three? I don't think so. "No, we don't have any names. Detective Harris has questioned some people, but she seems to think none were associated with the disappearances.   We've all but given up on trying to find those two men."

"That sounds like a pretty good idea Mr. Woods. Just a couple more questions and I'll let you get back to bed. Who's the tall man in the coveralls?"

"Coveralls?"

Yes, the man that you talked to at the Windmill Restaurant, Mr. Woods. I'm sure you remember talking to the man. You ate dinner with him. Remember?"

"Oh...yes, you mean Mr. Gonzalvez."

I knew you'd remember, Mr. Woods. Don't forget about that pretty faced schoolteacher. Now, tell me all you know about the man in the coveralls, this Mr. Gonzalves."

"Well, he used to work for the Dunlap's in Cashmere. He was their orchard foreman."

"Uh huh, so what did you and him talk about at dinner?

"Well, he knew that Christina and I were part of Detective Harris's team that was trying to find out about Brian Douglas's disappearance. He wanted to know all that we knew. That's it."

"You're smarter than I thought Mr. Woods. What kind of work did you do for a living?"

I knew that my alias was covered. "I worked for the government."

"Really. What did you do for the government?"

"I was a software engineer."

"No way," He gasped.

"What department did you work for?"

"ATF."

"Well slap me silly, Mr. Woods. I do declare. ATF! I'm impressed. I surely did under estimate you sir. ATF, Alcohol, Tobacco and Firearms, yes sir. There's more to you than anyone thought."

"There is no reason for you to be impressed. I was just a software engineer in a big computer atmosphere. Detail work. I wasn't out on the street or undercover, just a detail man on a computer. No need to be impressed."

Well, that about ends our little conference. I think I got more out you, than anyone thought, Mr. Woods. Yes indeedy."

I heard the paper being folded and then I heard a metal click. I had a small tape recorder and guessed he might have been taping our conversation. The chair scraped the floor as he stood. I felt something touch the back of my head...*a gun,* I thought. It was eerily quiet, and the sound of a hammer locking into place filled the entire room.

CHAPTER THIRTY-EIGHT

"Well it's been over a year since your mother vanished Natalie, and I feel very strongly you don't need to see me anymore." Dr. Janice Taylor suggested to the beautiful Natalie Hudson.

"I would still like to have lunch with you occasionally, Dr. Taylor."

"I would insist on it."

"The scar around my neck has almost disappeared and I'm not afraid to talk about it. My mother vanishes into the air, grandmother dies of a broken heart. You've done a lot to help me overcome this nightmare, Dr. Taylor. I couldn't have done it without you," I said and tightened my collar around my disfigurement.

"You've done that by your self, I'm glad you've started dating again. What's the name of that man you're dating Natalie?"

"Vanderbilt, but he likes to be called Vandy, Vandy Earhart."

CHAPTER THIRT-NINE

Detective Donald Jones hung up the phone and walked out to the reception desk.

"Sally, Randy Scott, the mayor of Cashmere is coming in and he's a hot head, very volatile individual. I think it's about Daphne Dunlap's vanishing. He doesn't like Tilden. He's bringing a mechanic with him that works on planes at Pangborn Memorial Airport, in Wenatchee. Have him come in as soon as he gets here, please."

"Yes sir?"

"He is excitable."

I knew when Randy entered the detective area before I saw him. He had a bullhorn mouth and a righteous entry.

"Come on in Randy," I yelled from my open door.

"This is Buddy Zeigler, a good friend of mine, Don," he announced as he stormed into my office.

I closed the door and waved them to the chairs.

"Sit down Randy, Buddy."

"You know Don, I've been trying to get John off his ass and do something about George Tilden. Personally, I believe he's responsible for Daphne Dunlap's disappearance. He wanted to be the DA in this town and when he gets elected...he sits on that big ass of his. What does he get paid for?"

"What have you got for me Mr. Mayor?"

"That's right, I am the mayor of Cashmere and I don't get any respect for it."

He stopped talking.

"I found some blood in the luggage area of George Tilden's plane a few weeks ago and happen to mention it to Randy," Buddy said quietly.

"Yeah, do you think we might be able to get District Attorney John Skundrich off his lazy ass and do something for a change, Don?" Randy railed.

"What were you doing in Mr. Tilden's plane Buddy?" Don queried.

"I was doing a yearly engine check."

"I assume you're a plane mechanic?"

"Yes sir."

"And he gave you permission to do this?"

"Yes sir detective, it's required by the state and the Feds."

Detective Don Jones was nodding his head. "Well I think we can get District Attorney John Skundrich to move on this Randy, but there are still procedures that we have to follow to do it."

"Yeah I know the stupid law and how it moves at a snail's pace. I just want some action or I'm going to waste the bastard myself," Randy railed.

"Be careful what you say Randy," Don advised.

The men stood. "Come on Buddy and let the detective go to work on this. Thanks Don. Would you keep me up to date on the happenings?"

"I will and thanks for coming in Buddy." I sat at my desk and thought about Stewart Woods. I finally had something to report even though this whole thing could be blood from a dead fish, deer blood or the dozens of people that George Tilden has had in his plane.

CHAPTER FORTY

I was sure I was going to get a bullet in the back of my head. I could feel the sweat under the hood that covered my head. Suddenly there was a loud knocking on my front door.
"You expecting anyone, Mr. Woods?"
"No," I gasped.
Again there was the insistent pounding on the door. I sat listening for what was going to happen. I never moved a muscle and then the doorbell began ringing along with the beating on the door.
"Do you want me to open it," I asked.
Nothing. I wanted to move my hands from my lap.
"Hello." I said as I reached up and took the hood off. He was gone. I turned the light on in the front room and hurried to the front door. I opened it to a short, bald man, in his skivvies, and a woman in a white robe with disheveled, gray hair.
"Hi neighbor, sorry to be such a bother but there's a skunk in our front room, and I'm afraid we've managed to scare it and it released it's stench in our house. Could you call the sheriff or somebody?"
Nearly killed by a low down rat and saved by a skunk, I grinned, still shaking as I called the police.

CHAPTER FORTY-ONE

Lorenzo Gonzalvez was thinking as he eyed his rearview mirror, that a truck had been following him since he left Wenatchee on his way home to Cashmere. It was a little past one in the morning and the traffic was sparse. Once Lorenzo reached the crest out of Wenatchee, the highway was void of houses for about six miles until he crossed the concrete bridge to his small cottage on the Dunlap ranch. He took his foot off the gas and allowed his Ford Ranger to slow to just forty miles per hour, hoping the truck would drive past him. It did. He watched as it maintained the sixty-five mile speed limit and quickly fell out of sight.

I knew I was jumpy because of all the undercover work I had been doing of late. Lorenzo thought. As I started across the bridge to Cashmere, I saw the truck parked across both lanes, blocking them. I looked in my rearview and saw that I was closed off behind me too. My headlights illuminated two men running toward my Ranger, each was carrying a handgun, with black hoods over their heads.

"Sir I need for you to get out of your truck and move quickly to the truck in front of you. NOW," he shouted, "and leave your keys in the ignition."

"Move, move," he yelled as he pushed me forward. I was directed into the back of the cab cover, with the big roll up door, I looked back toward my truck and saw that one of the men was driving it up behind us.

They drove a short way and then stopped. One of the men rolled the door open and placed a hood over my head. A man with a southern accent began talking to me.

"We're sorry about treating you like this Mr. Gonzalvez, but it was the only way we had of talking to you, sir. We're not going to harm you in any way. I just need to ask you some questions. There's a chair directly behind you, please sit down." We're going to secure your hands behind you. If you answer all our questions the way we want you to, then we won't be seeing you again. Do you understand that sir?

"Yes."

"Good. Now it's my understanding that you worked for Mrs. Delores Dunlap and that recently she passed away. Is that correct?

"Yes."

"Are you a Christian man, Mr. Gonzalvez?"

"There was a time."

"Then you know that Mrs. Dunlap's death was about the Lord's way. She died from natural causes. No one shot or strangled the good woman. In other words, we can't blame any living person for her death. Wouldn't you agree ,\\,Mr. Gonzalvez?

"I don't know about that."

"How's Mrs. Dunlap's daughter, Natalie Hudson doing sir? She's a mighty fine looking young lady. Miss Hudson's all that's left of that family. It would be a shame for something to happen to her."

"Nothing better happen to her," I snarled.

"Well, I'm going to leave that up to you Mr. Gonzalvez, only you can prevent that. Do you have any family around here, sir?"

"I'm an orphan."

"No wonder I couldn't find anything on you. In other words, no one would really miss you if you disappeared. Well, our little chat is over, so we're going to release you now. We won't be talking to you again. You'll find your car keys at the base of the third pine tree."

I could hear them whispering at the rear of the truck. I got the feeling they weren't through with me. One of the men stopped directly in front of me. He stood doing something and then I felt the first punch hit just above my right eye, and the second on the side of my head. After the eleventh punch the man was breathing hard and still he punched.

"That's enough," the man with the southern accent yelled. "Bring him over to the edge of the truck and place him on the ground."

I felt myself being lowered from the truck. My face hurt like hell but I was still aware of what was happening.

The man with the accent spoke, "I really didn't lie to you, Mr. Gonzalvez. I said we wouldn't hurt you if we liked your answers. I'm afraid I didn't like your responses."

"I think he's passed out," a man voiced.

Someone pulled the hood off. "I should have stopped you sooner. You might have broken his nose." The man with the accent proclaimed, he looks to be out cold. Lay him on the ground by his keys. Put the chair in the back of truck and grab the hood. Let's get out of here."

CHAPTER FORTY-TWO

"Thanks for meeting here, at Ohme's Garden, Mr. Gonzalvez. It's a little easier to see if anyone is watching us, plus it's serene and beautiful. I believe Chelan County maintains the grounds now. Nature is hard to enhance, but the Ohme's managed, with their humble, but lasting contribution, to do just that years ago. " I stared at Lorenzo's face as he took his sunglasses off. Some one had really worked his face over. Both eyes were still black and his nose was swollen. I could see he was serious.

"Things are out of control, Mr. Woods and I don't handle some one beating on me very well. I spent twelve years fighting wars and when Mrs. Dunlap offered me a job as foreman of her fruit orchards, I accepted without hesitation. I was fortunate to have worked in a similar situation as an orphan in West Virginia. I wasn't a foreman but I learned about fruit at that orchard. I've been very happy and content here until Daphne disappeared. Since then everything seems to be going to hell. I don't know you very well, Mr. Woods but I feel like you know more than you're saying. I don't mind that. You have your reasons, but I also believe that you want some kind of retribution from the same people that I'm searching for. I believe there are at least three individuals that are responsible for Daphne Dunlap's disappearance. I guess what I'm saying is, we both want the same thing. Mr. Woods, I was a damned good sniper for a little over ten years. I earned a lot of medals and I'm proud of that, but what I have in mind now is against the law. When I was a Seal I got medals for killing the bad guys. Here I would go to jail if I do what I want to do. My plans have changed because of what happened to me. They think they know who I am, but they're mistaken. I suppose I'm no better than those rats, but I do it for a better reason, I have a more noble purpose. That's *who I am* Mr. Woods."

Lorenzo was a man who did not mince words. He was now ready for action. Maybe this is what I had been waiting for all this time. *'Carpe Diem', seize the day,* I thought. I had been riding the fence for so long that it's taken Lorenzo to initiate the beginning of the end. Am I not the master of my own Karma? Is it really that hard to be me? To make decisions that so far have made people disappear and some drown; me with all my moral postures. Is Stewart Woods really any different than Brian Douglas? Could we be two different people?

While I was in the mountains, after my fall from the plane, I had no memory and no reason for retribution, no reason to seek vindication.

"Mr. Woods," his deep voice resonated, "I've made the decision that I'm going to eliminatae three men and then I'm moving to Brazil. They speak Portuguese down there."

My God, I thought and stopped walking. He took a few more steps and turned around. I stared at the man, aghast.

"You heard me correctly, Mr. Woods. You see the years I spent as a Seal, eliminating savages that killed for their beliefs is no different than this. The same as it was in Iraq or Afghanistan. The law prevails here and sometimes it benefits the bad guys. I'm just going to eliminate that possibility, and I'll still sleep well having done so."

"I don't know what to say."

"I guess I overestimated you, Mr. Woods. I honestly thought you would understand, just a gut feeling. Something told me you were after the same thing: justice. The word "kill" is harsh, especially when you're speaking about people, but these men are no different than the barbaric bastards I killed in the mid-east."

"I think we do have an agreement on what is justice. It's just that…well…it's so in your face; so blatantly honest. The reason I called you *was* to discuss this very thing. You just beat me to the punch, literally." I stood, looking at Lorenzo, willing his words to stop reverberating in my head.

"Do you have some kind of plan?" Lorenzo inquired after a few seconds.

"I do. I suppose you've been in a lot of planes and maybe helicopters, too?"

"Yes sir," he responded crisply, "in fact, sir, it has been a life long dream to learn to fly an airplane, and Mrs. Dunlap paid for my lessons and I am now able to fly. I'm saving money to buy a plane."

I paused for a few seconds, "Lorenzo would you meet me at Pangborn Airport tomorrow at the break of light…five thirty? You were right to go with your gut about me. I'm going to return your trust by telling you a secret that few people know about."

CHAPTER FORTY-THREE

Christina Palmer sat in her kitchen with Stewart Woods. "The truth Stewart, or Brian, or whatever your real name is, does it really matter? I haven't had a conversation with you in months. I haven't the slightest idea of what you've been doing. I'm not part of you anymore and I think you've lost interest in me. I can't force you to want to see me. Truth be told, I'm not sure I want to see you anymore. I don't have anyone else but I can't sit around moping about you. It's just not me. Having said all that, Brian, I really wish we could be a couple. I really like you."

I couldn't defend myself. I had been too immersed in my own problem. I was loathsome, despicable. It was all coming down on me and I don't think I could get any more depressed. It was my fault. I had been straddling the fence too long. I could have gone to the authorities when I first arrived back in Chelan and told them who I was and who I think tried to kill me. But no, I had to have vengeance. Over three years had passed and more people had died because I had no guts to do the right thing...or the wrong thing. I stood. I couldn't think of the right words to say to Chris. I don't think there were any words that would fit now and I couldn't face her anyway. I walked to the front door.

"Brian would you wait a minute please? I have something for you, " Chris choked out.

She set the box on the kitchen counter. "Please come over here and I'll show you."

She opened the box and I saw what appeared to be some kind of phones. She could see the confusion on my face.

"I bought these phones a little over a year ago, but I haven't seen you lately to give them to you. They really are very special because you can use them on your plane. It was my way of thanking you for teaching me to fly. It seemed like a good idea at the time because we could communicate while one of us was in the plane and the other on the ground. I would like to keep one of them in the event we ever start talking again. Would that be all right?"

She reached into the box and pulled out one of the units. "Look Chris…"

"Don't Brian, it's all right. Go. You don't have to explain now. Go do what you have to do. Get it over with…please," she appealed.

I walked out with the box under my arm.

CHAPTER FORTY-FOUR

Vandy Earhart had been to Cashmere to see Natalie Hudson and she had purposely avoided him. He was mad as hell and was looking for someone to take it out on. The car behind him had been driving with his headlights on bright. He tried speeding up and slowing down but the driver stayed on his tail. The first few miles he spewed out all the expletives that he could think of. When he finally pulled over and to his surprise the car behind him also stopped. Vandy jumped out of his car, trotted to the driver's door and jerked the door open.

"All right asshole I don't know what kind of game you're playing with me but I've had enough of it." He reached in to grab the man and the man took hold of his hand like a vice grip. He screamed in pain. The man stepped out of his car, with Vandy's hand still in his clench. He could now see a tall, muscular man, with some kind of mask on his head, wearing what appeared to be a wartime military uniform. Vandy could feel his strength from the grasp of his hand, and he easily turned Vandy around with the painful pressure, so that his right hand was practically touching the back of his head. Vandy gasped in pain.

The stranger opened his passenger door and sat Vandy down. He took out some handcuffs and put one on Vandy's left wrist, one on the handgrip above his head, climbed into the drivers seat, reached into the back seat, brought a black hood, placed it over his head.

"Why are you doing this to me? Who are you? Where are you taking me?"

The stranger started the car, turned it around so it was headed back to Cashmere without answering Vandy's question.

Fifteen minutes later the stranger stopped his car and dragged Vandy into a house, the hood still over his head. He sat Earhart on a chair next to a table.

"The woman's voice you hear next knows all about what you and the others have done, but we want you to admit it on this recorder." A tape recorder was turned on and a young woman's voice began talking.

"I have two questions for you Mr. Earhart and I want you to answer them with clarity and sincerity. Your life will depend on it. The man in your presence will be putting a noose around your neck as you answer my questions: I want to know what happened to Daphne Dunlap. Which is question number one. Question number two is: We want the names of the other men that helped you abduct Mr. Brian Douglas. You will have nine minutes to answer these questions, starting now.

The voice was familiar to Vandy but he couldn't quite guess who it was.

The stranger tightened the rope around the hooded Vandy and walked him outside. His legs were tied at the ankles. He was left in the sitting position on the ground. The man placed a twelve-foot wooden ladder next to a large pine tree, climbed up eight feet and threw the rope over a large branch. He pulled the rope down until Vandy was forced into a standing position and gasping for breath. The woman's voice stated, "You now have five minutes to answer my questions, Mr. Earhart."

"I don't know what happened to Daphne Dunlap," he whimpered, "honestly I don't know. I had nothing to do with her. That was Tilden's doing, and that's the truth. I don't want to die. I had nothing to do with her. I don't know what happened to her. I swear I don't know anything about her," he cried. "I don't know, I don't know," he whimpered, gagging.

"Who were your accomplices that helped you kidnap Mr. Brian Douglas?" the voice asked, "and now you have one minute to answer Mr. Earhart."

"Workman, Coangelo, Tilden and me," he screeched as the rope tightened and his feet left the ground. Earhart reached up over his head and pulled the rope to take the pressure off his choking neck. That's the truth," he gurgled, " George Tilden, Bart Colangelo, Tom Workman and me. We did it. Please, that's the truth. You wanted the truth, that's the truth. I don't want to die this way, please, that's the truth. We did it," he screeched. His arms were slowly losing their strength allowing the rope to once again tighten around his neck. He tried to raise his arms to the rope above his head but he was slowly losing consciousness.

Vandy could hear the tapping and as he opened one eye, he was aware that something was making the sound. He raised his head from the steering wheel ever so slowly as the rapping continued to his left. He coughed, was aware that he was slobbering and coughed again. His head ached.

"Sir, open up the door," the voice demanded "or I'll break the window."

Vandy tried to focus on the voice outside his window and could only distinguish it was some man in a uniform.

"Have you been drinking?" The voice shouted.

Vandy reached for the handle, pulled and fell out of his car.

The officer leaned down on one knee and smelled Vandy.

"Are you all right sir?"

"I'm alive," he anguished, "yes," grimacing, "I think I'm all right. What time is it officer?" Vandy asked, getting himself together mentally, his eyes blinking at the bright sun overhead.

"A little past ten in the morning, how long have you been parked here sir and I'll need to see your driver's license. Do you have some kind of health problem sir?" The officer helped Vandy stand and as he stood his legs wobbled precariously. The officer noticed the man had urinated in his trousers.

Vandy handed his license to the officer. The patrolman scanned his picture and returned it.

"You better sit down sir, before you fall down. Would you like me to call someone for you?"

"I'm all right just a little woozy, but I'll be all right. I'm under a doctor's care and I took some new medication that probably caused this," he responded and sat in the front seat again.

The officer got a call on his car radio.

"Are you sure you're all right Mr. Earhart, cause, I'm going to have to leave you."

"Really I'm fine. Thank you for stopping. I assure you I'm okay. Thank you for helping me."

The officer waved to him as he drove off.

Vandy stepped out of his car and tried to stretch until he thought his head was going to fall off.

CHAPTER FORTY-FIVE

"Thanks for meeting me here, Stewart, I fell in love with the Columbia River the minute I landed here several years ago. This valley, reminds me of my hometown in Portugal, only it's more beautiful here."

"Yeah, I agree this river does kind of draw you in. Now with all the dams that harness the hydroelectricity, it's productive too. It has this raw beauty, Lorenzo."

"Do you mind if we walk down to the picnic area?" Lorenzo requested, "I want you to hear something I recorded the other night."

The two men strolled down the short incline observing the manicured surroundings.

Stewart looked out at the lush green grass and all the beautiful flowers that surrounded the base of the entrance to the Rocky Reach Dam. They walked over to one of the green wooden tables that were randomly placed for the visitors to enjoy.

Lorenzo placed the recorder on the table, turned it on, and walked a few feet away.

Stewart remained transfixed to the metallic box, listening to every word.

After a few minutes, Lorenzo turned the recorder off.

Stewart Woods stood, walked a few steps and gazed out over the Columbia River.

"Well, there you have it Lorenzo. It has always been my contention that they were the culprits and that I would deal out justice to these no good bastards. You have given me the conviction to do what I have known all along but no guts to do it. Evan as I speak now, I know that I must do something that is not me. 'Thou shalt not kill," is a strong commandment. I'm not the staunchest of Catholics, but I have been a good member and I know if Father O'Reilly were here he would affirm that. Yet, as you have attested, they are bad people, no better than the Taliban in Iraq and Afghanistan."

"Mr. Woods, I think I know how you feel. A long time ago I might have had the same reluctance you're fighting. I want you to know, I have no such feelings. These men did something to the woman that I loved, not that she ever knew it. I would have worked for Dolores Dunlap for nothing. Natalie Hudson, the woman's voice you heard on the recorder, is Dolores Dunlap's granddaughter and she loved her grandmother. She and her grandmother were very close and she told me in confidence that she and Dolores felt Vandy Earhart was partially responsible for her mother's death. They had no proof, but after what I learned from Earhart, I was convinced he and the other three mentioned on the recorder were responsible. I know that you had met Daphne Dunlap and that you liked the beautiful lady. I too, have a reason to want to rid the world of these savages. I don't have any religion to thwart my feelings, only my training as a sniper to guide me. Mr. Woods, you only need to give me the word and I will eliminate them, only too gladly. It's up to you sir."

CHAPTER FORTY-SIX

"Vandy where are you? You're not making any sense. Have you been drinking? What do you mean Lorenzo Gonzalvez knows all about Brian Douglas. Where are you calling from Vandy?" George repeated.

"He was going to hang me George and if I hadn't told him about us he would have killed me," He blathered in a drunken slur.

"What are you talking about? Who is this Gonzalvez character? Are you home right now? He knows what about us?

There was a long pause as George Tilden sat, frustrated, in his office.

"It's all over for us. I had to do it. Yeah George, I've been drinking and I guess I'm drunk, otherwise I wouldn't have called you. I spent eight years in the pen and I'm not going back. This wasn't the perfect crime we thought it was. We shouldn't have beat up the Portuguese man, George. He's pissed and I know he's coming after us and he is one bad dude."

"Let me come and talk to you Vandy. Where are you?"

"It's too late, George. It's too late, too late," the phone went dead.

George immediately called Bart.

"Bart go to Vandy's house and see if he's there."

"Why do I want to do that George?" Bart asked suspiciously.

"He just called me and he's drunk and talking nonsense. Get over there right away and I'm going to his office to see if he's there."

George met Bart at the Loop, where they sat at an open park bench.

"Where do you think he called you from George?" Bart asked.

"I don't know, I checked the tire shop. It was closed. He had been drinking and he wasn't making any sense. Were you aware that he had done some time in a prison? He said he wasn't going back to that. Do you think he has the guts to…?"

Bart studied Tilden's worried face. "If he does, it will be one less worry. What do you think we should do, George?"

"We have few options."

"We should have killed them when we had the chance, now we're on the defense. What about the southern dimwit you hired that was suppose to get rid of Stewart Woods? Scaring off that big Portuguese soldier didn't work out very well, either," Bart whined.

"This isn't the time to cast blame Bart. Let's figure out what we should do and we better do it fast."

The following day the Wenatchee World had a picture of the tire shop owner, Vanderbilt Earhart in the paper with a short story about his suicide.

"Did you see the paper this morning?" He asked Bart on the phone.

"We're not out of the woods yet, George."

CHAPTER FORTY-SEVEN

I was not comfortable with Lorenzo Gonzalvez assisting me in what I was going to do. Now I was forced to ready my plane and commit immediately to the elimination of George Tilden and Bart Colangelo. In a way I suppose that's good. I was glad to read in the Wenatchee World that the police department had deduced a probable suicide for Vandy Earhart. I was sure Lorenzo took notice of the article in the paper, though he never voiced it.

As I drove up the hill to my rental I wondered how Lorenzo had obtained entrance. I parked, looked up at the almost full moon. It was a clear night, no clouds. This was it. Once I get to my rental, there is no turning back. I was scared and wondered what I would tell Christina. I opened the door and stepped out into the night air. It was cool but I was sweating a little. Nerves I guessed. I walked up the sidewalk and my mind went back to the mountain cabin where I had spent over six months recuperating. At that time, I had very little memory of why I was there, except to know I was in very bad shape. The gentle giant of a man, Tom Wah Gee was nursing me and living a lonely reclusive monks life. He would never entertain the thought of killing someone for any reason. At least I don't think he would. In reality, I never really knew the man, except that he appeared to be a good person. Now it seemed like a lifetime ago.

I returned to my car and sat. Lorenzo bringing the two criminals to my home had caught me off guard, but I would make it a positive intrusion. I drove home. The last time I had a conversation with Lorenzo, we had agreed that he would not be complicit in my retribution, but obviously he had not been sincere. I found him sitting at my kitchen table drinking coffee.

"Lorenzo, I thought we had gone over everything that I want to do. In order to live with myself I have to do this on my own. I appreciate all your input, but this has to be my call. I will be totally responsible if things don't work out."

"I'm sorry Mr. Woods. My word is usually good. I will promise that after this thing is done, I will leave the area and you will never see me again. I *have* to do this with you because they came after me too. You saw what they did to me. Besides, I have my own personal reasons aside from being stubborn, it's who I am."

I poured myself a cup of coffee and sat down across from him. Our eyes met and I could see that he would not budge from his position.

"What time do you have?" I asked.

"Twelve sixteen."

"You're sure no one saw you bring them here?"

"There were no lights on any of your neighbor's houses, except the one at the end of the block, but I didn't see anyone," Lorenzo responded.

"Where did you put them?"

"In your garage."

Stewart frowned, "Did you happen to check the time you got here?"

"I believe it was around ten forty five. Yeah, it was ten forty five. I had checked my watch with your kitchen clock."

"How long will they be out?"

"At least two hours, maybe three," Lorenzo nodded.

"Well, I'm all gassed up and have alerted the night watchman that I'll be leaving around two this morning."

"Whose the night watchman?"

"Ole Toby Gillespie, I think he's been there since they built Pangborn Airport," Stewart smiled.

"Yeah, and he still takes his plane up occasionally," Lorenzo nodded.

We sat quietly drinking our coffee. I glanced across the table at Lorenzo. I could understand that this might be like one of many firefights he had been through in the ten years he had been a Seal. The man had no conscience. Yet he appeared to be normal in all the other ways. He had been given an honorable discharge from the Navy; loved someone and felt the pain of lost love; been a good employee, never drank in excess by his own admission and had a clean record with the law, according Detective Don Jones.

Though I knew very little about this unique individual, he had managed to earn my total respect by just being who he was, honest, direct and loyal to his values.

"Well, I guess we might as well get started. I'll be back in a few minutes. The only lights that I saw were on the city's street lamps, down below. Let's load them up in your pickup and get this done," Stewart ordered.

The Chacker Bellcraft slowly lifted off from the ground and steadily climbed to a thousand feet when it coughed and then sputtered. Lorenzo met Stewart's eyes.

"I think we better turn around Lorenzo and go back to Pangborn. Sounds like a fuel pump. What's your guess?"

He nodded, raising his thumb up.

After landing, they emptied the aircraft of its passengers and stored them in the back of the hangar bay. Stewart called Todd Nelson, his mechanic.

"Todd agrees with us. He has to wait for the shop to open at eight this morning to purchase another fuel pump, so he won't be here until nine or nine thirty. Can we keep the two under until then Lorenzo?"

"No problem," he responded and walked back to where the two men were stored.

Meanwhile Stewart called Christina Palmer.

"I can't believe you're really going to do this terrible thing Stewart," Christina said anxiously. "Turn them over to the proper authorities and let them pass judgment on what they did to you. If you carry out this thing it will haunt you the rest of your life...please Stewart don't do this...you'll be paying a terrible price. Father O'Reilly wouldn't want you to do this. That Shuai-lin monk wouldn't...you haven't broken any laws, you can still turn them over to the police. Do you still have the special phone I bought for you in your plane?" She waited for a response, but got a dial tone instead. "Oh crap," she shouted, with futile exasperation and laid the phone down on the kitchen table.

"Rev her up Mr. Stewart and hold it for two minutes," Todd requested. For two minutes the engine held a steady hum. "Sounds like she's good to go. You can be on your way sir," They shook hands and the mechanic left the hangar.

Lorenzo and Stewart secured the two passengers in the back of the plane and once again they were at a thousand feet, flying west to the Cascade Mountains.

All was quiet, except for the steady hum of the Continental engine.

"Do you have a specific area in mind for these two?" Lorenzo inquired dispassionately.

"I do. We're going up to Canada beyond Vancouver." Stewart responded.

The phone that Christina Palmer had given Stewart rang. Stewart looked at the phone and then at Lorenzo.

"It's my girlfriend," Stewart responded.

The phone rang and kept ringing until Stewart hit the switch to answer.

Christina could hear the drone of the engine and knew that Stewart could hear her voice.

"Where are you Stewart?" she beseeched. He didn't respond. "I know you can hear me because I can hear the plane's engine. Are Tilden and Colangelo still in your plane? Please talk to me Stewart. Have you already done what you said you would do to them? Please Stewart talk to me? Listen please, I'm at the police station and Detective Jones is here. I told him everything you told me about your abduction and that you now know it was Tilden, Colangelo, Earhart and Workman. He knows everything Stewart. You don't have to do anything bad," she pleaded, "even the District Attorney is here, please listen to me," Christina wailed. Suddenly the phone went dead. Christina froze with the phone in her hand. Her gaze directed at the D.A. and Detective Jones in disbelief. Stewart had turned the phone off.

"They're awake Stewart," Lorenzo barked out, as he stepped over the seat and crawled to the back of the plane. "Do you want me to bring one of them forward now?"

Stewart nodded and yelled back, "yes."

Tilden was dragged forward where Lorenzo had removed the passenger seat. Tilden's head was where the seat had been. He was looking up at Stewart. Stewart could see the fear in his eyes as he peered down from the captain's seat at him. All the years of angst had built up and led to this very moment.

"Do you know who I am Tilden?" Stewart growled fiercely.

Terror gripped Tilden and he could only stare in hypnotic cowardice. He thought he now knew, but was afraid to even think it. It couldn't be, it just couldn't be. He was dead, no way this man was---it couldn't be him, but...

"That's right," Stewart shouted in a frenzied rage. "I am alive and I'm going to do to you what you did to me, and since the weather is better I'm going up a couple thousand feet before you fly," he screamed and laughed psychotically.

After climbing up two thousand feet he set the plane on autopilot, stepped around the Captain's seat and in the process, inadvertently hit the switch to the phone Christina had given him.

Christina was still seated in the Detective's office, and when she heard the drone of the plane, she hurried out to alert the DA and Jones that she was in contact with Stewart's plane again. They rushed in just in time to hear what sounded like Stewart's voice just above the thrum of the engine and the wind of an open window or door.

Hardly distinguishable, "I'm going to show you what it looks like before you experience the reality of it Tilden," he yelled above the engine and wind as he dragged him to the open door. He stood Tilden up and held him in the doorway. Tilden was white with fright. Uncontrollably he urinated in his pants and drool ran down his chin. The uncompromising wind lashing it back to his face and slapping spittle on Stewart's forehead.

"I don't want to die," he choked, coughing, blithering that he was sorry for what he had done to Brian Douglas.

"Tell me what you did to Brian Douglas you liar, you coward," Stewart yelled in his ear. I want to hear what you did to him. I want you to say it you bastard."

"I did it, we did it," he screamed, "I confess, I did it, I admit it, please don't do this to me. I don't want to die," he spewed out, tears streaming down his face. Stewart turned his head and saw that Lorenzo had Bart Colangelo standing close by. He directed Tilden back to Lorenzo's grip and brought Bart, hands tied behind his back, to the open door, holding him by his right arm. Bart's eyes met Stewart's and he defiantly shouted, "I'm not going to beg for my life, I have no regrets about what we did to you, and I'd do it again. I'm not going to rot in some jail for what I did. In a flash Bart head butted Stewart and both stumbled sideways, bodies thrashing uncontrollably, Stewart still clutching Bart with his left hand, and his right arm flailing for something to grab hold of. The two fell awkwardly across the captain's seat and Stewart's right hand inadvertently hit the autopilot. The plane slowly started to list to the right. The men crashed against the opposite door and Lorenzo sprang into action trying to get to the captain's chair and the controls. Tilden slid down the side and sat on the floor. The centrifugal force pushed Bart and Stewart against the closed door and held them there as the plane began a nosedive toward the ever-nearing forest below.

Christina had placed the phone on Detective Jones's desk while they all listened to the drama aboard the out of control plane, all hypnotically glued to the sound of the spiraling engine and gushing wind as the plane's nose plummeted toward the sea of pine trees on the landscape below. Then as quickly as the phone had been turned on, it went dead.

Christina stared, transfixed at the small soundless electronic machine, tears suddenly welling and then raining down her cheeks.

After a few minutes, Detective Jones stood, walked by Christina, patted her shoulder and left his office.

"I'm sorry Christina," District Attorney Jack Skundrich said, almost in a whisper, as he left the office.

"How long has it been since...since?" Heidi Latham asked solemnly across her kitchen table of Christina Palmer and Loretta Workman.

Loretta eyed her. Christina lifted the coffee cup to her lips.

"This Wednesday it will be exactly one month since the radio went off in Brian's plane," Christina responded dispassionately. Tears welled in her listless brown eyes. Loretta reached over and took Christina's hand in hers.

Heidi stood, walked to the counter and retrieved some tissues.

Christina took one and dabbed her eyes.

"You would think by now I could talk about it without all the tears," she lamented.

Loretta stood and walked to the counter and brought the box of tissues to the kitchen table.

"First I lose my son and now I guess Bart has fallen to the same fate, and I still don't know why," Loretta sighed as she wiped her eyes.

"No news is still good news, girls. It hasn't been proven that the plane crashed. I admit, a month is a long time. But look, didn't Brian disappear for a year before you knew he was alive, Christina?" Heidi spoke, sounding somewhat positive.

Christina looked up and smiled ever so slightly at Heidi.

"That truly was a miracle, but how many miracles can we count on. We've played that tape over and over and it sure sounded like...like well, it just doesn't change," Christina despaired.

"You think they would have called or at least notified the Wenatchee Police Department by now if they were alive," Loretta chimed in.

"Maybe they can't for some reason we don't understand," Heidi responded.

"Like what?" Loretta challenged.

"Maybe they pulled out of the nosedive and crashed and they were all knocked unconscious and they're in some hospital in some small town and unable to talk," Heidi shot back.

Loretta looked at Christina and smiled. Christina's face turned into a big grin and she began snickering, which inspired Loretta and Heidi and all joined in a spontaneous, stressful relieving laugh.

"Maybe an angel plucked them from the plane and placed them in a farm house that has no phones and the people that live there are unable to speak and their neighbors are miles away," Loretta guffawed.

That brought another round of laughter.

"Maybe some Indians that live in the Cascade Mountains have them hidden in some tepee and no one knows their whereabouts," Christina piped in, and again they chuckled at their whimsical catharsis. The laughter had released the tension.

"How about a shot of Jack Daniels," Heidi whispered mischievously.

CHAPTER FORTY-EIGHT

Stewart landed his rental plane in Cashmere. The trip had been quiet and contemplative. Lorenzo was satisfied with the conclusion of the whole ordeal and George Tilden remained alive only by nodding and hardly discernible grunts. His massive stroke had left him but a whisper of the man he had once been. One side of his body remained limp and useless: the other listless, only slightly better.

Stewart rented a Ford SUV and escorted George Tilden in a wheel chair to the passenger side and Lorenzo lifted Tilden into the front seat.

As they drove silently toward Wenatchee, no one spoke. Stewart mulled over in his head, the last landing he had made. The evergreen trees destroyed his plane, as he tried to land on a small meadow in Canada. The crash had evoked a heart attack on Tilden. He and Lorenzo only bruises and some sore ribs. They considered the demise of the man. Lorenzo had argued that they terminate him and initially Stewart had agreed. But then as they waited for the doctor of the small town in Canada to determine if Tilden would die from the massive cardio infarction or live, Stewart's morbid determination tempered significantly and his Catholic upbringing came to the forefront. Reluctantly Lorenzo did concede. Now as they reached the crest of Highway 2, Wenatchee in their sight, Stewart called Detective Donald Jones and informed him that he and Lorenzo Gonzalvez would be bringing George Tilden in for American justice. Bart Colangelo had fallen out of the plane as it spiraled to the ground.

Tilden attempted to speak. His voice garbled, incoherent, with meaningless babble.

Stewart turned his head slightly to the back seat, "Did you get any of that Lorenzo?"

"No."

Tilden barked out the same sounds again and when no one responded, tears welled and ran down his cheeks.

Lorenzo leaned forward from the back seat and wiped Tilden's face.

"We're sorry we can't understand you George," he said earnestly.

Stewart reached across and touched George's shoulder with a gentle squeeze.

Stewart and Lorenzo had discussed George Tilden's ordeal for the last few weeks and summarized, he would probably never see the inside of a prison cell, however justice would prevail.

In Father O'Reilly's words, "Hell is living with the knowledge of the wrong you have done."

Also available by Joseph Montoya

The Shade

ABOUT THE AUTHOR

Joseph Montoya lives in the San Francisco Bay area of California, but writes about the town in which he spent his formative years, Wenatchee, Washington. The town has the distinction of being called the 'Apple Capital of the World', which it is of course. All the neighboring towns are small, with apples, cherries, pears, peaches, and a variety of different fruits being the main industry, though grape vineyards seem to be making their presence felt in the surrounding areas. His books are all fiction/mystery.